# THE TRUTH GAME

# THE TRUTH GAME

## Joyce Dingwell

G.K.HALL &CO.
Boston, Massachusetts
1990

First published 1978.
© Joyce Dingwell 1978.
Australian copyright 1978.

Published in Large Print by arrangement with
Harlequin Enterprises BV.

G.K. Hall Large Print Book Series.

Set in 16 pt Plantin.

*Library of Congress Cataloging in Publication Data*

Dingwell, Joyce.
   The truth game / Joyce Dingwell.
      p.   cm.—(G.K. Hall large print book series)  (Nightingale
series)
   Originally published: London : Mills & Boon Limited, 1978.
   ISBN 0-8161-4967-4 (lg. print)
   1. Large type books.  I. Title.
[PR6054.I54T7   1990]
823'.914—dc20                           90-32429

# Chapter One

EXACTLY on time the Sydney to Hong Kong jet put down at Kai Tak Airport.

Alighting with the other passengers . . . and Kit . . . Honor, who only a few moments ago had caught her breath at the wonder of Hong Kong from the sky by night, now caught her breath again at city sounds, strange smells, new sights, different people. But most of all she caught it at the continued close presence of the man beside her. 'Christopher Blyth,' the owner of the fingertips touching her elbow had told her, 'but answering to Kit.'

It seemed incredible to Honor that this morning at the Sydney Terminal she had never heard of a Christopher Blyth, but destiny . . . or the reservation office . . . had seated them side by side, and the journey that Honor had miserably expected to

1

be filled with guilt because of Danny had turned out instead to be an unforgettable, quite glorious escape.

At least that was what she had said to Kit, and he had looked deeply back at her and probed: 'Escape? But surely you can see that I'm already a prisoner.'

'Prisoner?' she queried.

'Your prisoner.'

'Oh, you idiot!'—Darling idiot, a voice inside of Honor had added.

'I'm serious,' he said.

'You couldn't be.'

'I am. I *am!*'

'Look, you won't even see me any more,' she protested.

'I will,' he assured her.

'Hong Kong is a big city, I forget how many million people.'

'But only one girl in a million.'

'You say nice things, Kit,' she smiled.

'My heart says even nicer. Lean closer and listen.'

'A big city . . . you won't even see me . . .' Honor had repeated breathlessly . . . hopefully. She had warmed to this charming man at once.

'Of course I'll see you. Where are you booked?'

2

'The Odetta.'

'I know it.'

'Is it good?' she asked.

'Very good . . . but only good for one night for you.'

'What do you mean, Kit?'

'One night only, Honor.'

'But I've reserved a room for a week until I find digs.'

'*One night.* Tonight. Tomorrow I'll take you somewhere less hotel-ish.'

'A hotel has to be hotel-ish.'

'I know the very place. There are three girls there now, and looking for a fourth to help with the rent. Hong Kong rents are high, alas.'

'The girls may not want me,' she pointed out.

'They are part of my circle. Oh, yes, they'll want you. You said you had a job?'

'The Bright Sun Emporium.'

'I know that, too.'

'Quite the Hong Kong man,' Honor had teased.

'Well, this is my second term here. What will you be doing at Bright Sun?'

'Mr Hing, the proprietor, was over in Sydney recently buying some of our artifacts to exhibit here, and he met me, liked me, then decided that an Australian in his Hong Kong display centre might be an advantage.'

'You would be an advantage anywhere, and don't tell me I say nice things again or I'll——'

'Yes, Kit?'

'My answer to that would be a promise, not a threat,' he had smiled back. He had reached for Honor's hand, found and pressed it, and Honor, heart racing, had left her hand there.

And now the journey was over. The two of them had eaten together, drunk together, sat through a film together; they had talked, they had lapsed into silence, they had slept, occasionally they had looked down on banks of clouds, fluffy white clouds, smooth silver-grey ones, towards dusk sheer rose-gold. At evening they had shared a star.

'It's been wonderful,' Honor had said as she had obeyed the final seat belt order.

'It's been magic,' he had agreed.

'I think I almost forgot about Danny,' Honor had admitted. She already had told Kit bits and pieces about Danny; she had confided more to him than she had confided to anyone. Because of that she had not been surprised when he had answered grimly:

4

'*I* won't be forgetting that young man if I ever meet up with him. Except that you tell me he's your brother——'

'Actually a half-brother.'

'And a no-good half-brother, I'd do much more than not forget.'

'But he's not like that at all, Kit, not a no-good, he's—well, he's Danny.'

'Also the reason you've run away to Hong Kong?'

'Yes.'

'Then I suppose I shouldn't hate him, at least he's brought me you.'

'Oh, Kit, he hasn't . . . I mean, he couldn't . . . I mean, it's too soon to know.'

'Mere words, Honor?' The man Honor had been placed beside had looked long and deeply at her, and Honor had felt herself melt. Yes, only words, she had realised, words without foundation, for she did not feel like that at all, not with this dear Kit. She felt . . . yes, she felt . . .

'I'll let you relax tonight,' Kit had told her. 'Jet lag can occur even in a run like this. But tomorrow——'

'You'll have forgotten.'

'Never. *Never.*' Still close to her, Kit finally relinquished her to the Odetta porter, who was waiting for the hotel guests beside an air-conditioned bus.

'Tomorrow,' Kit called. He touched his hand to his lips, then nodded the action to Honor.

But Honor did not respond. She could not. He *will* forget, she had been thinking. Out of sight, out of mind, it's only been an enjoyable—but casual—encounter for him, a passing kind of thing. But she knew she would not forget.

She sat back and the bus began its perilous journey through the teeming city streets to the Odetta Hotel, perilous because Honor had never seen so many people and so many vehicles at the same place at the same time in all her life.

The big hotel lobby when she reached it was full of people—people arriving, people leaving, people being collected for a night life tour of Hong Kong, people just sitting and looking, for there certainly was plenty to watch.

Honor was whisked to the sixteenth floor, bowed into a pleasant suite, shown the air-conditioning knob, the bell for iced water, then . . . with another bow . . . left alone.

She went straight to the large window, a window full of navy plush harbour now alight with gleaming big ships, sparkling smaller boats, bobbing sampans and junks. It all made for a shining mosaic, a band of fire, she thought, entranced. Aloud she thrilled: 'I'm in Hong Kong. I'm here . . . and so is Kit Blyth. We're both here together.'

She looked a long time, then she realised her weariness and crossed to the bed.

'Goodnight, Danny,' she whispered gently, for she always loved him in spite of his million faults. Then:

'Goodnight, Kit.'

She slept.

She awoke to a morning like no other morning in the world, or so she thought. Nothing unusual in her room nor, going by the silence only punctuated by the distant regulated purr of smooth-running lifts, in the hotel. No, outside. Definitely . . . after Honor had crossed to the big window again . . . outside. The street below was literally crammed with every variety of vehicle that could be driven, pushed, wheeled or coaxed along, and all raising an ear-splitting noise. There were opulent cars, busy utilities, painting trucks, bicycles, tricycles, rickshaws, hand-barrows, perambulators, push-carts, motor scooters, cases attached to wheels and tugged, boxes simply dragged along the ground.

Besides the traffic there was the biggest number of people, excluding a public rally, that Honor had ever seen. Policemen directing, Chinese blandly disobeying them, schoolchildren in snowy white uniforms darting dangerously between oncoming cars, ayahs waiting decorously for safe crossings because they had the custody of a small child, pedlars taking the opportunity of every traffic pause to sell their wares.

Every colour of humanity. The rather hot pink . . . for it was a torrid day already . . . of the American, Australian or English tourist, the range from deep cream to burnt gold, according to their territory corner, of the Cantonese, the coffees and chocolates and olives of other races.

Behind the traffic and the people were the shops—and such shops! Everything, as Mr Hing had told Honor, from monkeys that ran up sticks to exquisite silks, from delicate blouses to matched golf sets, and the stores housing them bearing the most amazing names: 'Zing-a-ling' . . . 'Sweet Bye and Bye' . . . 'Inn of Dear Bliss' . . . 'Happy Harbour'.

Beyond the shops stretched public reserves, rather tattered grass, but the tatter of use and not neglect, and on the grass more people again, but people doing gymnastics. Nothing strenuous, nothing violent, but long, lissom, graceful movements. Unconcerned with their fellow exercisers, the people bent and flexed. Honor watched delighted at a band of shadow boxers, at a young family of father, mother and two small children doing their limbering up together. The father was slim and studious-looking, the mother as neat as the gilt pin in her coiffure, and the children, the boy bullet-cropped, the girl with a windowpane cut to her blue-black hair, quite exquisite.

'Lovely,' enjoyed Honor, feeling like running down and joining them herself.

She was turning her attention to the harbour—Hong Kong Harbour, meaning Fragrant Harbour—when there was a knock on the door. She crossed the room and opened up.

The Cantonese steward who had settled her last night bowed and held out a cable. Was Missy comfortable? he asked. Was the warm hot enough, the cool not too cold? Would Missy like breakfast in her room or would she take it downstairs?

'Here . . . downstairs . . .' Honor mumbled indistinctly, not aware that the steward must be sadly confused.

But he was evidently practised in the ways of guests, for he smiled and said he would bring along some tea.

'Yes, tea,' Honor said absently; she was looking at the cablegram she had been handed and now had opened. It was awfully long for a cable, it must have cost Danny a fortune, for from Danny it had definitely come; Honor had checked that at once. *And fortunes were something that Danny had not.*

She went to her bed and sat on it. Anything from Danny always needed something on which to sink after you had faced up to it. She sighed and read.

'ABSOLUTELY ESSENTIAL YOU DO WHAT I ASKED YOU TO DO STOP MATTER OF LIFE AND DEATH STOP COME HOME OR I MUST COME UP TO YOU STOP HELP ME STOP PLEASE HELP ME STOP SOS SOS SOS. DANNY.'

'Oh, Danny, Danny!' Honor despaired.

Suddenly, in this foreign hotel room she was instead in her home town in Sydney, and her stepfather was talking to her in a low, serious voice.

Her mother had died very recently, and

10

there was a mutual pain in them as they spoke wistfully of Gwen.

'But,' Lindsay Breen had said carefully, 'it won't be long for me, Honor. You see, dear, I'll soon be with her again.'

Honor recalled looking up to the step-father she had come to love as though he was her own father.

'You mean . . . you don't mean . . . no, you can't . . .'

'Yes, Honor. It can't be that much of a surprise. One look at me and you must have known I wasn't intended for old . . . that should be older . . . bones.'

Honor *had* noticed, but, hopefully, she had put the thought aside.

'Only two things . . . no, I should say two people . . . worry me,' her stepfather had gone on. 'Danny, naturally. Then you because of Danny.'

'You need never worry about Danny, not while I'm around,' she assured him.

'That's the real thing that worries me, Honor, you've always loved that rogue too much.'

'Our lovable rogue. Yes, I expect I have.'

Honor now remembered her first meeting with her half-brother, a rather uncertain mother, uncertain of her little daughter's reaction, a plainly uncertain stepfather, then —love at first sight. Honor had loved the baby at once. She loved him now, now after all he had done, and she supposed wryly that her love, just as her stepfather had warned, had been, and was, too much.

'He'll break your heart, Honor,' Lindsay Breen had said that day, 'Danny is that sort. He's sweet, he's winning, he's entirely irresistible, but at the same time he's lamentably weak. He leans. He depends. He's a taker, never a giver, He's——'

'He's your son, Lindsay.'

'Your half-brother, Honor.'

'My *brother*. Oh, yes, I love him even that much. No halves here.'

'I know, I know, dear, and that was why I had to speak. That foolish love of yours. You're four years older than he is.'

'Danny is twenty, I'm twenty-four.'

'Watch him for me some times, Honor, *but not all times.*'

'All times, Lindsay,' she said firmly.

'He'll use you.'

'Danny,' Honor recalled answering, 'is the using sort.'

'If he meets the right girl it might help,' Lindsay sighed.

'It might, but until then——'

12

'Until then you'll be the victim. Stand by him—but don't let him strangle you. Resist when the need arises. For the need will come. I know my son.'

'And I love him,' said Honor. 'But I promise you that I'll bow out when Danny asks for too much.'

'I'm leaving all I can for him, but in your keeping, that is, until he's a man, a proper man. However, it's not only money that worries me, it's your attention, your sacrificial concern.'

'You're exaggerating, darling,' protested Honor. 'Just as you are exaggerating about yourself. I'm sure *you* will be dealing with Danny, not I dealing with him, for many more years.'

'Not even many more months, Honor.' Lindsay Breen had added: 'Not even weeks . . . days . . .'

He had been right. He had died soon after. And Danny, the little boy who had been put in Honor's arms twenty years ago, had come to her arms for comfort . . . later for more comfort . . . then more. In a short while he had dominated her life. He had demanded, insisted, coaxed, sulked, done many abominable things, but through them all Honor had excused him, restored him, protected him—until this final thing, his latest demand, presented, as usual, in a gentle low key manner, preparing the way to a bigger onslaught. For certain reasons, very important reasons, urgent reasons, he had told her, he wanted, *he must have* his half-sister—married. Married to a man of his own choice.

'*What?*' she had gasped.

'Listen please, Honor,' he begged.

'I'll do nothing of the sort! This time you've overstepped yourself, Danny.'

'He's all right, Sis, in fact nice, it'll be quite okay.'

'Danny, you're off your head!' she exclaimed.

'Actually I am, Sis, with worry. You see, I've kind of promised him.'

'What?'

'I had to. Honor, you must believe me, I *had* to. I had no choice.'

'Well, there's no choice now. You will not, now or ever, decide whom I marry, Danny.'

'But—I've said so.'

'You mean it isn't just a kind of promise but the real thing?'

'Yes, I mean that. I was definite, Sis.'

Honor had wheeled on Danny. 'What is

14

all this? What is it this time? Tell me at once!'

But Danny hadn't. He had kept repeating wretchedly how terribly important, how vitally important it was to him. In fact there was no other way out.

'I think you're meaning no other way out for you, Danny.'

'Yes,' he muttered.

'Way out of what?'

'I can't tell you, except that it's——'

'All-important?'

Again Danny had mumbled: 'Yes.'

'You've done something,' she accused.

'I didn't mean to.'

'You never mean to. All those big bills you ran up, you never meant to. That car you "borrowed" and crashed, you never meant to. I helped you then, Danny, but I won't . . . won't, I tell you . . . be part of this. What are you playing at, Danny? Marriage broker? What's the fee you're asking for me?'

'I even wish it was like that,' Danny had blurted, 'but it isn't, it's far worse.'

'Tell me,' Honor insisted.

'I can't.'

'If you can't, I can't help.'

'The only way you can help is by agreeing to what I ask . . . what I *beg* of you.'

'No, Danny.'

'He's decent, he's quite a good chap, and besides——'

'Besides?'

'Marriage isn't like it used to be, you can—well, you can back out afterwards quite easily these days.'

'It's still no, Danny.'

'Honor, it can't be no.'

'No, no, no!' For the first time Honor had turned away from Danny, had left him standing there.

He had tried again . . . again . . . He had become more pressing, more urgent each time. At last it had come to Honor that both of them were getting nowhere. For Danny's sake as well as her own she must get away.

Not for all time. She could not have borne that. To shut the door on Danny would have been like an amputation on herself. But she would remain away for as long as it took for Danny to come to his senses. In that spirit she had accepted Mr Hing's offer, accepted it without a qualm, for Mr Hing was the respected father of five lovely daughters, and his lovely wife, who always accompanied her husband on his business

16

trips, was as anxious to have Honor as was Mr Hing.

'A golden sprig of wattle among our dark windflowers,' the Hings had said poetically, which sounded very nice, Honor had thought, for straight tow hair.

She had obtained a passport, booked a seat, then had left. Not a word to Danny, not a hint, but . . . looking down at the cable . . . little good it all had done. Danny had promptly discovered her address, no great problem for Danny; he would simply go to the firm where she had worked, use his charm, and get it with a smile, an indulgent nod, and at once. That was Danny.

Once more Honor read the cable, fragments of it, the important, significant bits.

'Absolutely essential you do what I asked.'—That meant the preposterous marriage. 'Come home.'—Oh, no, she wouldn't, not now. 'Or I must come up.'—Oh, no, not that either.

There was a knock on the door, and involuntarily Honor stifled a small cry. Not—not Danny already!

She stood frozen, and there was a second knock. When she didn't answer that, she saw in horror the handle gently turning. How dared Danny . . . how dared he . . .

The door swung wide open. Two men stood there. One was the steward with the promised tray of tea, the other was——

'Kit!'

Honor ran blindly forward, aware only of a vast relief. Oblivious of the steward she went to Kit's arms, and as unaware the man she had met in the plane held her tight.

The steward went softly out.

## Chapter Two

WHILE Honor mopped up her tears, Kit read the cablegram.

'He's no good,' he said when he had done.

'You said that before, Kit.'

'Well, I was right, wasn't I? He's simply no good, my dear. Now drink up your tea and we'll be off.'

'Off?' she queried.

'That flat I mentioned. I've been in touch with the girls and they're overjoyed. Honor, *drink your tea*, don't water it.' For Honor was crying again.

'It's relief,' she said, 'even if it is only the temporary variety.'

'Temporary?'

'Danny will still come, and Danny will still find me. That's Danny.'

'And this is Christopher.' Kit crossed to Honor. 'He won't find you,' he assured her. 'We'll leave no address. But even if the hotel knew it, the Cantonese are instinctively a close and proper people, they never speak out more than they have to, and never without permission.'

'They told you where I was,' she pointed out.

'Where you are is different from where you've gone.'

'Perhaps you're right, but perhaps, too, they've never encountered a Danny.'

'Encounter?' Kit said a little oddly. 'Tell me, Honor, do you know some other male in this Eastern city?'

'No . . . oh, yes, Mr Hing.'

'This was not Mr Hing. He was a westerner—tall, rather flinty.'

'I don't like the sound of that,' said Honor uneasily.

'I didn't like the look of him, I don't go for the hard, whipcord type.'

'Was he?' she asked.

'Very much.'

'But how do I come into it?'

'I enquired for your room number at the desk and he came alive—very visibly alive. He was standing a few customers up, settling some account possibly, and he turned at once and stared at me.'

'Then it was you he was interested in.'

'You haven't let me finish. He stared at me *speaking your name*. Honor, I suspect you have a secret admirer in Fragrant Harbour already.'

'If I have, I don't know him.—Kit, look at that charming boat.' Honor pointed to the shining harbour and a mock old-time brigantine that was crossing between the Victoria side and Kowloon.

'That's the *Tak Fu*. Tak Fu interprets to something resembling One Million Blessings. But just now, Honor, *my* blessing cup overflows, for I have one million and one.'

'One more than a million?'

'Yes. You.'

'You are sweet, Kit,' Honor smiled.

'I am when I'm with you. Are you finished? Then gather your things and we'll move off. When do you start at Bright Sun?'

'Mr Hing left the date open in case I had travel lag, but I think I'd like to begin quite soon.'

'I'd like that, too, because I begin again

20

quite soon myself, and I don't like leaving a girl like you around by herself.'

'No one would even turn a head,' Honor shrugged.

'A tall flinty gentleman did even at your name.'

'Then there must be two Honor Jasons.'

'At Hong Kong at this particular time of the year? At the Odetta Hotel?'

'Yes, it is odd,' she agreed.

'Very odd. But not to worry, you won't be found where I plan to hide you away.'

They descended in the lift, then left the cool lobby for the burning heat of the street. Hong Kong got it both ways, Kit said as they gasped at the simmer level of the sidewalks—it sizzled in summer, it froze in winter.

'But it's always exciting,' defended Honor, for already she had fallen in love with the place.

'Yes, always.'

'And always beautiful.'

'Not in typhoon time, or the time of the rains.'

'Heavy rains?'

'You could never imagine them. We'll grab this rickshaw.' Kit beckoned a rickshaw boy and they both climbed in. 'It's

21

my favourite way of travelling when I have a fair companion,' Kit grinned, 'it makes for a far closer settlement, a smallish seat like this has to.'

'How many fair companions have there been?' asked Honor.

'A few, but no more from this day on.' He put his arm round her shoulder. She relaxed against the arm, then, intrigued in spite of her worry over Danny, she looked out.

This, then, was Hong Kong. Not the Hong Kong of Mr Hing's poetic description, which had compared his beloved city to the touch of fine silk, the feel of jade green water, the song of windbells, but a rather tatty Hong Kong of strong smells, perpetual movement, crowd and crush of people, clang of cars.

There also should have been the clop of wooden pattens, but Mr Hing already had told Honor that nowadays you only saw pattens in the rural areas, the people in the city wore European dress. But occasionally, Honor noted with enjoyment, a cheongsam crept in, an embroidered kimono. She felt sorry for the young, very beautiful girls, for denim, the same as with the rest of the world, had pushed aside brocades and satins, made them less the flowers that they really were.

She heard an ejaculation of annoyance from Kit, and turned her attention away from the street to look at him.

'That fellow I told you about . . . the one at the hotel desk . . .'

'Yes?'

'I'm sure I just saw him again.'

'Where?'

'In a taxi. There . . . no, that one.' Kit nodded his head.

Honor followed the direction of the jerk, and saw a taxi to their right but a little behind them. In the passenger's seat sat a man who certainly filled Kit's description of tall and flinty. Even as she looked the man looked back at her, looked so briefly it could scarcely be called even a glance, but Honor had the unpleasant feeling that for all the brevity the fleeting inspection had missed nothing.

'Know him?' asked Kit.

'No.'

'Sure?'

'Certainly I'm sure.'

'Honor, you are being straight with me?'

'Straight?' she queried.

'You're not using me, you're not running

away from this fellow and he's following you?'

'I've never seen him before in my life, Kit, and the only one I'm running away from is Danny.—Kit, where are we going?'

'Down this ladder street . . . they call these steep alley cuts ladder streets . . . somewhere where he can't follow, not in a car.'

'If he is following.'

'Well, it looks like that to me. He was certainly interested when I said your name, and that look just now was scarcely unseeing.'

'But you still do believe me that I've never seen him before?'

'When *you* say it, yes . . . but has he seen you? Does he know you?'

'If so, I don't know how.' Honor felt upset, and her voice showed it. At once Kit was sorry and said so. He took his arm from the back of her shoulder and slipped it round her waist.

'It's nothing. Don't worry. Look, there he goes now.'

Honor looked up from the lower level of the ladder street and saw that the taxi was certainly moving on. She heard Kit confidently order the rickshaw boy, who was really a dried-up little old man, to climb to the top again, then take the first turn to the right. Because of his boyish glee she did not have the heart to correct him when he declared that they had lost the pest. For they had *not*. Honor had glimpsed the taxi drawn up behind a concealing stall, concealing because of the masses of clothes hanging on every side of it. Now she saw the taxi move off again . . . move off behind them. She saw the hard, flint man. No, she didn't know him, but no, she wouldn't worry. Certainly, too, she would not deflate dear triumphant Kit who was still claiming a victory. She turned her attention once more to the buzzing streets, calling to her escort to look at the cane cages of mock canaries done in yellow silk who sang sweetly at the turn of a key, at bowls of young snakes for sale for special dinners, and Kit smiled at her absorption, then presently said: 'We're here.'

'Here' was a four-storeyed block, which was considered high enough in Hong Kong, Kit said; only the luxury hotels tried to touch the sky. The flat was on top, which was very handy for watching the lower flat dwellers come out on their balconies of a morning to exercise.

'I saw them limbering up in the park this morning,' Honor nodded.

'Yes, but a busy worker usually only finds time to come out on his balcony. Only Natalie will be at home now, she's an air hostess on the Philippines run, away several days, back several days again. Nita and Averil are secretaries, nine-to-five girls. You'll meet them tonight.'

'I want to start being a nine-to-five girl myself, Kit. Do you think you'll be able to tell me how to get to Bright Sun from here?'

'We'll have a practice run after you've settled in,' he promised. He paid off the rickshaw boy. 'Sorry there's no lift, Honor, but walking keeps down the rent.'

'I don't mind.' Honor had glanced up and down the street before she had stepped out from the rickshaw, and there was no taxi in sight, so evidently they had lost 'Mr Flint'. Although she had decided to take no notice of him, the knowledge that he was not there any longer helped her in some inexplicable way, inexplicable because a complete stranger like he was had no right to intrude into her thoughts.

'I don't mind at all,' she repeated.

'That's my girl—and Honor, I mean what

I say when I say that, so don't begin your too-soon-to-know routine again.'

'I won't,' Honor smiled.

She accepted his outstretched hand and together they started on the four flights of stairs.

The door of the unit after Kit had knocked was opened by a small, brown-haired girl. She had a particularly sweet face, and Honor warmed to her at once.

'You're Honor,' the girl said.

'Yes.'

'I'm Natalie, but Nat will do.'

'You are the air hostess?'

'Yes.' A grimace, which Honor questioned rather incredulously. Such a glamour job, she commented.

'But I'm not a glamour-minded girl.'

'No,' laughed Kit, 'our Nat would sooner be at home with a family and a husband.'

'The husband first,' Nat smiled, 'then the family can arrive. You see' . . . to Honor . . . 'I was an "only", and now I feel—well, deprived.'

'It does happen,' Honor nodded with sympathy; even in her present anger against Danny she could not imagine life without her brother.

'Except that I have other ideas' . . . Kit

flicked a significant look at Honor . . . 'I'd offer my services, young Natalie. Failing me, any ideas?'

Nat dimpled. 'Plenty. In fact I have him all mapped out. I'd rather like a dependent man, depending on my love and confidence in him, I mean, not financially.'

'You really mean you want to mother him,' Kit claimed. 'Know anyone, Honor?'

'Perhaps I do.' Honor was thinking of Danny. She was thinking of what her stepfather had said. 'If he meets the right girl it might help.' Often she had thought the same way herself. A right girl might be the *only* way to help Danny.

'This is our corner, Honor,' showed Natalie, 'you'll be sharing with me.' She had opened the door to a small but pleasant room with a tiny balcony. It was plainly furnished, but Nat had added bits and pieces from both Hong Kong and the Philippines, and the additions had brought it to life.

'It's charming,' said Honor.

Kit meanwhile had the kettle on, and presently he called: 'Tea!' There was not only tea but a selection of appetising cakes and buns.

'They have good pastrycooks here,' he explained. 'No doubt they got it from the

28

English, I know of no other Eastern city that goes in for such four o'clock delights.'

'It's only ten o'clock,' Honor laughed.

'Then give me back that cake.' Kit took it and bit where Honor had bitten. 'It's all right,' he grinned to Nat, 'we're in love.'

It would have been fun had not the slightest of looks crossed Natalie's sweet face . . . a quick, uncertain look. But at once she was smiling and saying: 'Kit, you are a fool.'

'After you unpack, Honor, I'll take you round to the Bright Sun,' said Kit. 'Bright Sun is where she'll be going to the saltmines, Nat.'

'Lucky you, Honor.'

'Said by someone up in the clouds!'

'Said by someone whose influential uncle got her into a much sought-after job but who would sooner be on the ground selling saucepans.'

'Will I be selling saucepans?' Honor asked.

'No, you'll be put on a less mundane section, but Hings do stock saucepans, they're an emporium and sell everything.'

They talked until all the pastries were eaten and the tea drained, then Honor unpacked while Kit read the paper, then they

29

both went out again, this time in the direction of Bright Sun.

'Do you work near here, Kit?' Honor asked, taking a mental note of each twist and turn to Bright Sun.

'Yes, but I live across the harbour at Victoria, which is only a ferry ride away, quite cheap, exactly a mile and a frequent service. Here we are now.'

Honor regarded the building critically, but the same as the way she had felt with the Hings, she could find no fault. It was solidly constructed, and Mr Hing had resisted the Cantonese weakness of over-embellishment with lights and symbols. The sole adornment it wore was an illuminated Bright Sun.

'I'll leave you to it for an hour,' said Kit, 'then come and get you. But don't try to look round by yourself if you're out earlier. Lots of the streets lead nowhere, there are blind crescents and dead-end half-moons of lanes by the score. If you do manage to get lost . . . but don't, or I'll practise that promise-threat on you once more . . . then make your way to the harbour. A street rims it, and you'll soon get the general pattern of the city again. Best of luck, girl.' He grinned, touched her hand and went off.

Honor climbed several imposing stairs, pushed a large imposing door, gulped gratefully at the air-conditioning, then walked down a red carpet to a pretty Cantonese girl behind a reception desk.

Within minutes . . . seconds . . . Mr Hing had been buzzed. He emerged from his office at once, all smiles and bows. He was enchanted to greet Miss Jason. How wonderful of her to contact him so soon.

'I want to begin soon,' smiled back Honor. 'In fact' . . . looking round the excellent displays . . . 'I can't wait.'

'You flatter us,' bowed Mr Hing. 'I thought I would give you an island stand here. Would that suit you or is it too public?'

'I'm proud of our crafts and I want to show them,' Honor assured him.

'Our many clients, and we do have many, will be enchanted to see them, hear about them from a lovely Australian girl. A coincidence!' The Cantonese clapped his hands.

'Yes, Mr Hing?'

'We have with us at this very moment an Australian gentleman, though I could say an Australian Cantonese gentleman. Mr Rowan has been attached to Hong Kong so long one almost thinks of him as Cantonese.

31

He is not, of course, though his aunt, very aged now, was born on one of our gems of islands.' Mr Hing waved in what Honor supposed was the direction of the sea. 'Her parents were British, and stationed here, but when the time of service was up they stayed on. The child, now this aged aunt, never left here. All this is a long time ago, and the gentleman with us today is not really a nephew but a great-nephew.' This time Mr Hing waved graciously to somewhere nearer, and Honor, following the wave, froze.

It was him, the man who had so annoyed Kit by showing immediate interest when Honor's name had been spoken at the hotel desk, the man who Kit suspected had followed them, and who Honor knew, not just suspected, had done so, because she had seen him quite plainly.

'You must meet Mr Rowan, Mr Hugh Rowan,' Mr Hing said. He gave Honor no opportunity to decline, no chance to manufacture an excuse, within minutes he had them together, and was making a long flowery introduction.

At the end of it Honor said coolly: 'How do you do?' but her greeting was positively effusive compared to his uninterested, non-committal, bored and patently antagonistic:

'Madam.'

Fortunately at that moment Mr Hing was called away, he would have been upset at the chilly atmosphere and undoubtedly made it worse by trying to instil some warmth.

The man, too, 'Mr Flint', or rather Mr Rowan as Honor knew now, had turned away. He did not even nod to Honor as he opened and then went out of the big front door.

The receptionist came up to Honor and said in a rather worried voice that Mr Hing would be tied up for some time, but would like Miss Jason and Mr Rowan to browse together . . . the girl looked around unhappily for the tall Australian . . . and Honor nodded, and began unobtrusively to edge towards the back of the building. She had noticed when she had come in that there was a back exit. She would use that, come round the street and wait for Kit where he had said he would pick her up again. By going the back way she would give 'Mr Flint' full time to be well off the scene. She certainly would tell Kit all about it, but not immediately; it would be a pity to spoil an otherwise pleasant day by including *him*. By this time she had slipped out of Bright Sun into bright sun. Very hot bright sun. Honor felt her make-up running at once. She also felt a little light in the head after the cool emporium.

She took a left turn, then turned right again. This should bring her into Cameron Street to which Bright Sun opened its front door. It should have, she knew some moments later, but it didn't. Too late Honor remembered Kit's crescents and half-moons that led to nowhere. This seemed to lead to nowhere. She took another turn that did a complete circle, another turn the shape of a wedge of pie. After that she knew she was lost.

'If you get lost, make for the harbour.'

Honor recalled that, and asked a direction. Ninety-nine out of a hundred Cantonese understood English, she had read, but Honor could only pick the hundredth. When she had done this five times, she began pantomime. Swim. Yes, they understood that, but obviously they did not couple swim with harbour, for each time they pointed to a tourist bus running out to some bathing bay.

34

Then Honor remembered ferry . . . Star Ferry.

Yes, they knew that, and they pointed the direction. Either it was the heat or Honor's weariness by now that made the walk much further than she liked or wanted, for by the time she had got there, and realised the length of the harbour-rimming street, she felt quite sick.

She stood a giddy moment wondering what would happen if she keeled over, which was what she felt she was going to do very soon. Already the buildings around were swaying, the street coming up to meet her, the——

'This way.' The voice cut through her dizziness, but barely so, the hand on her arm directed her but only faintly so because she was almost beyond feeling, but the sudden coolness of a hotel lobby steadied her enough to keep her from falling, steadied her, anyway, until she was lowered into a chair.

'Tea.' Now the voice was directing a waiter. 'Jasmine. Cold.'

To Honor the voice said: 'Cold is not as the Cantonese like it to be partaken, but you need something in you very quickly. I believe you've become dehydrated, an easy thing for a newcomer to these hot suns. Take a long gulp when it comes and then sit quietly back. Sit back now.'

Honor did.

Slowly she found her senses returning, and she opened her eyes. The hotel to which she had been brought was very old, very dignified, very mellow. Best of all, in her present condition, it was cool and dim. She sat on, taking things slowly, noting the hotel's potted palms, its elaborate caryatids, the bellhops in old-fashioned pillbox caps. A handsome relic of a former era, she recognised . . . and then she recognised something else. She recognised the voice of her rescuer now directing the pouring of the tea. It was 'Mr Flint'. Mr Hugh Rowan. The piece of ice Mr Hing had introduced her to, the man Kit had objected to . . . and she had as well.

But just now there was no objection in Honor. She took hold of the long glass when it was handed to her and put it to her mouth.

'Drink it all,' he ordered.

Again Honor did as she was told.

He did not hurry her, and she did not hurry herself out of her lethargy. Indeed, she could not have done so, and she admitted it humbly.

'Don't worry, it takes time to get acclimatised,' he told her. 'Hong Kong can be hotter than Hay, hell and Booligal . . . you, as an Australian, would know that line of verse . . . but contrariwise in winter it can make Iceland seem a cosy place.'

'How do you know I'm an Australian?'

'I know.' His voice had an unexpected harshness after the comparative mildness of his weather discourse. 'What are you doing down here, if I may ask?'

'I was lost.'

'You weren't when I last saw you.'

'I had to meet Ki—someone, and I got lost.'

'You had to meet him by the harbour?'

'No, in front of the emporium.'

'Then, good lord, all you had to do was walk out of the emporium, wasn't it?'

'Yes.'

'But you didn't, did you?'

'No.'

'Because you didn't want to meet me?'

'I had already met you,' said Honor.

'Because you didn't want the person you were to meet to see me?'

'No . . . yes . . . I mean . . .'

'You've answered me,' he shrugged.

A moment went by, then Honor demanded angrily: 'Why should I want Kit to meet you?'

'Is that his name?'

'Yes. Also why should Kit want to meet you himself?'

'My reply to that is why not?'

'You followed him in a taxi. You spied on him.'

'Oh, no, not at all.'

'But you did ! I saw you.'

'I wasn't following or spying on *him*,' the man said blandly.

'Then?'

There was no reply.

Honor had raised her eyes to the man's eyes; they were blue eyes, she found, blue ice, she had never seen eyes so cold before.

'Then you have something against me?' she asked.

'Your words.'

'But your thoughts?'

'Shall I call for more tea?'

'No, I feel better now,' she assured him. 'I'll go.'

'Go where?'

'Back to the emporium. Kit said if I

pinpointed myself from the harbour I should have no trouble in finding it.'

'So Mr Hing has not yet finished with you?'

'I don't know about that, but I do know I'm to meet Kit there.'

'Boy meets girl,' he nodded, 'or in this case is it girl meets boy? Tell me, as a matter of interest, do you always make the first advance?'

'I beg your pardon?'

'I won't repeat it, instead I'll change that "girl meets boy" to "girl meets boys". Plural. You seem to have a talent for masculine scalps. How do you come to have so many strings to your bow?'

'What on earth are you talking about? No, don't explain, it would only be insulting mumbo-jumbo.'

'Not mumbo-jumbo,' he refused, but he did not disallow the insulting. 'There goes the *Tak Fu*.' He pointed to the picturesque brigantine now crossing the harbour. Framed by the hotel's quite lavish grand windows, with their Georgian preponderance of scrolls and velvet hold-backs, the boat was a wonderful sight.

'One million and one blessings,' Honor

39

murmured, then clapped her hand to her mouth. 'One million,' she corrected.

'I think . . . to someone . . . it's what you said at first, a million *and one.*' He smiled fulsomely and it was distasteful to Honor. 'How nice to be girl meets boy.'

'Before, you said boys,' she reminded him.

'Yes, I did.'

'Why did you?'

He did not answer, instead he looked at his watch.

'I don't know if you arranged an hour to meet this person, but getting lost and having tea on the strength of it hasn't made time dawdle.'

'No, I must get back. Thank you for your help. I'll find my own way.'

'And be a nuisance to someone else? Oh, no.' The man signed a chit, pressed something into the waiter's hand, then led the way to the rotating door. 'I'll come with you,' he said.

'I don't want you.'

'Nonetheless I will come.'

'Ki—my friend won't like it.'

'He won't know. I'll deposit you and then leave.'

'Suppose he's already come and left?

You did say it was later than I might have thought.'

'Then you'll be lost again, won't you? We turn here . . . turn here again. There you are, the Bright Sun. You must have walked a mile to the harbour when you could have got there under several hundred yards.'

They proceeded in silence, nothing was offered from either of them until the emporium was reached. Then:

'I'll leave you,' the man bowed politely, and crossed the street.

There was no Kit waiting, and for a moment Honor believed she *was* lost again. Then he appeared, smiling, repentant. He had run into someone, he said, an old friend, and time had slipped by. Had Honor been waiting long? Forgive, forgive.

Honor laughed . . . said she had only just arrived herself, then was thankful that Kit did not pick up that 'arrived' and ask from where she had come.

She got into step beside him. Girl meets boy . . . boys . . . that man had said. Why had he challenged that?

But she was glad Kit was there, she had not even ascertained the flat address, and it

41

would have been an embarrassment to be in the same predicament a second time.

. . . A second time? As they started walking she glanced across the street, she looked idly, never expecting what she saw.

For the man was still there, whether to check them or whether to be on hand if she repeated her previous lost performance she did not know.

Uncharitably, for his purpose could have been sincere on her behalf, deliberately she walked even closer to Kit. Girl meets boy, he had said . . . tell me, he had also said, do you always make the first advance?

On an impulse she tucked her arm in Kit's arm, and when Kit, encouraged, turned and kissed her, she kissed him back.

*Well*, 'Mr Flint'?

## Chapter Three

KIT and Honor looked at shops for a while, took a ride on a bus top, had coffee and *deem-sums* on a roof garden, walked through a park, then at last made for home. When they got to the unit it was dusk, a warm, blue dusk, and the other two girls had arrived back from work.

Kit introduced them . . . Nita friendly and easygoing, Averil a little guarded and slightly withdrawn. Averil smiled at Honor, though, and extended her hand, then began talking at once in a faintly challenging voice. She announced that she and Nita had invited their current boy-friends for dinner . . . a quick glance at Kit . . . one in Customs, one in Air Control.

'Air Control should suit our air hostess,' Kit inserted.

'Leaving what for me?' It was Averil, and sharply.

'My dear Av, shouldn't that what be whom?'

They all laughed, but Honor found the mirth a little strained somehow. She thought the girls seemed nice, but she knew it would be to Nat she would go to confide things, from Nat that she would value confidences.

Natalie, meanwhile, was looking very doleful. Nita told Honor that Nat always looked like that when she was about to report back to work.

'So nice for Nat to have found her true vocation,' teased Nita. To Honor she said: 'The dear girl's an idiot, she has the most promising job in the world—I mean, where

43

else do you meet millionaires, top executives, very important, and possibly eligible, people?'

'It's wasted on her,' Averil took up. 'All she does is put herself out for travelling mothers. She heats all the babies' bottles, changes the little pets, and all for a sticky kiss, not even a bottle of Chanel. Once' . . . Averil rolled her eyes . . . 'she even brought a child home. Seems Mamma wasn't well, so Nat took it upon herself to give her a break from junior.'

'Benjamin was a beautifully behaved baby,' defended Nat.

'We all know that, darling, you've reminded us a dozen times. There's no doubt Benjamin left his mark on you. Also' . . . a grimace . . . 'five fat greasy fingermarks on our new velvet divan.'

However, Averil's virulence was mostly put on, Honor guessed. She felt sure both girls were quite fond of Natalie. She looked at the brown-haired girl in her tangerine uniform, and again, unbidden, she found herself thinking of Danny.

It was a pleasant dinner. The boys, who arrived soon after, were good company, and the conversation never lagged. At half past seven Kit and Honor drove Nat to the Kai

Tak Airport, and after they had said goodbye for three days Kit suggested a run up to the Peak.

'Don't we have to cross to Victoria first in the Star Ferry?' Honor asked.

'Not if we have a car. Nat has left me her car until she comes back, so we'll cross by the tunnel. It's quite a thing, the under-harbour tunnel.' As he told her, Kit had joined the city traffic again, choosing a lane that would take him to the tunnel approach.

After they had emerged from the tunnel, Kit elected to leave the car at the bottom of the Peak, and, instead of taking the steep curved road to the top, to ascend by cable tram.

'Because,' he said, 'everyone should approach the Peak for their first time from the cable.'

The tram began its rattling journey upwards, accompanied every inch by squeals of fear and joy.

'Tourists,' Kit grinned, 'they're either scared or enraptured. Locals don't notice the scenery or any change of grade.'

Up, up, they went, Honor doubting a little nervously if the cable tram could climb any higher. Then Kit said: 'This is it. All

45

out!' He jumped down and swung Honor after him.

Together they went to the parapet.

'*Love is a Many-Splendoured Thing* was filmed here,' Kit said softly. 'Do you wonder?'

Honor, looking down, did not wonder, and said so in an awed voice. The glittering mosaic beneath her was so brilliant, so scintillating, it seemed a pulsing ball of fire for as far as the eye could reach. Across the mile strip of water to Nine Dragons, or Kowloon as it was now known, the lights of ferries, junks and sampans shone like fireflies.

'Beautiful?' It was Kit in her ear.

'Yes . . . yes!'

'Like you are?'

'Oh, Kit!'

As naturally as a flower turning to the sun, as sleeping, waking . . . living, Honor turned, like a flower, to the warmth of his kiss.

When they went down to the car again, crossed the tunnel and came back to the flat, it was time for Kit to catch his ferry home.

'I'll have to change sides,' he said a little

crossly, 'all this going and coming is no good.'

'You've been to the Peak before,' Averil reminded him thinly. 'You should have learned by now that you can't do these things in five minutes.'

'These things?' Kit's eyes were narrowed on Averil.

'You heard me, Christopher.'

'The trouble with a circle,' Kit said to anyone who was listening, 'is that you're public property.' He gave Averil a cool look and asked about the boys.

'Gone. They're working men.'

'And I'm a working woman,' came in Honor. She felt a little confused. What had Averil meant when she had said: 'You should have learned by now'—and why had Kit given her such a chilly look?

But there was no chill in Kit's farewell to Honor.

'I'll see you tomorrow . . . hear all about it.' He drew her out into the small hall and kissed her again. For Honor it could have been on the Peak a second time, with the stars as witness.

Promptly at nine the next morning Honor reported to Mr Hing at Bright Sun. At

47

once he gave her the enjoyable task of arranging her own display.

She did it with extra care; the other displays were so excellent she knew she had stiff competition. However, even though she could not emulate the delicate embroideries that were offering, the exquisite carvings, the story-telling fans, she knew from past experience there was always public interest in the native Australian art she had to show, and the interpretations she could give to each article, from tales of the Dreamtime to the present time, from fantasy to fact.

Also not just the first black man but the first white ones, for a group of undergrads, who had gathered round Honor, soon touched on Australia's first white settlers in their keen questions.

If, they asked, the early settlers lived so far from any civilisation as Honor, on a map she had brought, had shown, how had they remained civilised? For example—marriage. White men always had embraced the practice of marriage, so how had marriage been performed out there? In some remote places it was known that a man used to lead his woman to the top of a mountain and there declare to all the world that they were now husband and wife. Had it been like this in early Australia?

'No mountains,' smiled Honor, 'or very few, and it was not like that. The early form, according to one account, was this: The man and his chosen mate would find a stream and together they would throw in a very heavy stone. If the very heavy stone did not float to the top they were considered married, and married they remained until the stone rose from the stream bed. Of course if a travelling pastor managed to reach them, they were conventionally married, but that sometimes was never, or quite often some seven or eight children later.' She added with a smile: 'The marriage stone still on the bottom of the stream.'

The story was a great success, and Honor had to retell it throughout the morning. It was only on the last occasion that she felt confident enough to let her attention wander; she had been so anxious to do well on this, her first occasion, that she had entirely absorbed herself in her job. But now she looked around, and saw a taller figure than the rest of the listeners in the row at the back. It was Hugh Rowan, Kit's 'Mr Flint'. She flushed as she realised he must have been listening to her account, but not lis-

tening as the others had listened, with delighted interest. No, 'Mr Flint' would listen
with his cold blue slits of eyes half-closed,
his mouth thinned.

'Congratulations on your praiseworthy
aiming to please,' were his first words
after the crowd had thinned and he had
come forward. 'People respond to a concoc-
tion like that.'

'Except that it was not concocted.'

'Oh, come!' He permitted a brief disbe-
lieving smile.

'It was not!' In spite of her determination
to be cool Honor spoke hotly. 'As a fellow-
countryman you should know something of
Australian legend.'

'I've spent more of my life out of Australia than in,' he told her.

'Spent it here in Hong Kong.'

'Actually no, but on one of our many
islands. My great-aunt has a home there.'

'Which will one day be yours.' She said
it casually, without much interest, but his
quick response was anything but casual or
disinterested.

He looked at her quickly and narrowly.
'Are you trying to be naïve?'

'Naïve? Why do you say that?'

'Because you already know all about it.—
To whom it could pass.'

Honor could not follow him. Did he
mean that presumably she had learned this
from Mr Hing? Well, she had—in a way—
she had learned about the old aunt and
the island on which she lived, but how did
that small knowledge make her naïve . . .
naïve in that meaning tone of voice?

'For a man who spends most of his time
on an island you seem to spend a lot of time
in the city,' she observed coolly.

'I have to—just now.'

He was staring very intentionally at her;
it was a cool deliberate look.

'I have work to do.' Honor, bewildered,
angry at his veiled talk, not following the
trend, turned away.

'By all means.' He turned as well.

For the rest of the week Honor did not
see Hugh Rowan, and it made for her enjoyment. A message had come from Natalie
that she was delayed in Luzon and would be
away another three days, so Kit took further
advantage of the car.

They drove out to the New Territories,
climbed hills and stared across at lands
now in the possession of Communist China.
They examined duck farms, had delicious

51

dinners on floating restaurants, drove to the Tiger Balm Gardens, swam at Repulse Bay.

On every occasion Honor got to know Kit better . . . and like him more. It was good, she thought, to like someone as well as love them, for already she felt she loved this man. He was always charming, always completely disarming, perhaps he was a little on the extrovert side, but if so he was a gay and winning extrovert, he made everything seem exciting, he made everything seem to move to a dancing beat.

Most of all Honor loved his words to her; they were always extravagant, always thrilling.

'The days have been matched pearls since I met you, Honor,' he had said, 'matched to match you.'

She no longer spoke of time and it being too soon to know, for time no longer existed, and she felt sure she knew.

Yes, it was love.

But for all her happiness, Danny still intruded. Danny, she knew, would always push through. She could no more shut Danny out of her heart or her life than she could—well, even tolerate Hugh Rowan. Now why had he come into her thoughts? She had not seen him for a week.

52

Then Honor saw 'Mr Flint' the next day, but because at once she stood back in a doorway he did not see her. He was entering the Odetta Hotel. Perhaps when he was in the city and not on his aunt's island he stayed at the Odetta. But this time he did not stay long. He was scarcely in than he was out again, almost as though he had gone there only to make an enquiry. Honor still stood back, and in the end in all fairness she had to buy a set of wind-bells from the shopkeeper. She could have bought prettier ones from Bright Sun at a cheaper price, but she paid cheerfully. It was worth it to learn a little more about 'Mr Flint'. Now she knew he came to the Odetta Hotel. For what? Or should it be for whom?

When Natalie came back from Luzon the girls threw a party. Any excuse was excuse enough for a party, Honor suspected. She also suspected that a party was the last thing that Natalie wanted.

'It's been a hectic week,' Nat sighed to Honor. 'I was hoping for a little peace and quiet.'

'When the crowd goes you'll get it,' promised Honor. 'The girls will pair off, and you and I can have a quiet chat and then go to bed.'

'What about Kit?'

'Kit doesn't live at Kowloon, remember, he has to catch the ferry back to Victoria.'

'It would be nice to talk,' brightened Natalie.

Everything went as Honor had told Nat it would. The noise was deafening, but in time it diminished and all but the three men left.

'I can't stop long,' grumbled Kit, envying the other two who had rooms quite close, 'I really will have to scout round for a this-side dig.'

'Or find a that-side lovely instead.' It was Averil, speaking apparently casually, but her words cut into a conversation pause, cut quite sharply, and for the briefest of moments there was a hollow kind of silence. Honor, who during the exchange had looked down on her hands and felt a little embarrassed, raised her eyes again and surprised a cold exchange of glances between Averil and Kit. At once Averil looked uncomfortable, but Kit looked angry. But scarcely had Honor registered the looks than the looks were not there. Perhaps they never had been there at all.

'Thanks for the good advice, Av,' Kit was saying with his usual charm, 'but I already have my lovely.' He smiled at

Honor, a special smile that, in spite of that unguarded moment between Averil and Kit, went straight to Honor's vulnerable heart.

Kit went reluctantly, then later the boys left. Nita and Averil went to bed, then afterwards Natalie and Honor, whose turn it was to tidy up after the party, went as well.

'A party I could have done without,' sighed Nat in the little balcony room.

'They meant it to cheer you up,' proffered Honor.

'Also to have a party,' Natalie laughed. 'They're both party girls.—Honor, did you hear a knock?'

Honor hadn't, and said so.

'It was a subdued one, as it should be at this time of night, but it was still a knock. There it goes again.'

'I'll see to it.' Honor was not yet in bed and she reached for her gown.

'No, I will. You're a stranger here.' Natalie borrowed Honor's robe and was out of the door before Honor could object.

Honor heard soft voices, heard the door closed, heard quiet steps to the kitchen, a click of a light. Then the voices began again, barely audible, Nat's gentle tone . . . someone else's. Someone's voice Honor *knew*, but it was too quiet, since a door was closed between the bedroom and the kitchen, for her to recognise.

Next there were steps and Natalie returning, opening and then closing the door behind her.

'Honor, you have a visitor. I've explained to him that the others are in bed so he must keep his voice down.'

'His voice?' she queried.

'It's your brother, Honor, your brother Danny. I'm afraid he's very upset.'

'Oh, yes,' said Honor grimly, 'he'd be upset.'

Nat ignored this comment.

'He seems a nice boy,' she appealed, 'quite a dear boy.'

'Danny is when it suits him.'

Nat passed that over, too.

'So don't be hard on him . . . hear him out.'

'At two o'clock in the morning!'

'Be kind to him, Honor, he's quite—well, distraught.'

'Oh, Nat, Nat, Kit was right when he said you were a compulsive mother,' Honor sighed wryly, holding out her hand for her gown. 'Don't worry, I won't do to him what he richly deserves.'

'And you'll listen?'

'I'll listen.' Already Honor was opening the door.

A few moments later she was listening and wishing she could not hear.

But that came afterwards. Immediately came the instinctive reaching out to Danny, his instinctive response to her. For whatever had happened, was happening, would happen, they still loved each other like brother and sister, and for several moments they just stood and clung.

Honor composed herself first.

'Danny, how are you here? Why are you here? Who told you where to come?'

'The first answer is no trouble.' Danny attempted a swagger, but it was rather a pitiful effort. 'I flew.'

'On what?'

'A jumbo.'

'I'm not joking, Danny, far from it. I meant *how?* How did you get the money to come?'

'I go to work—remember?' he muttered.

'Perfectly. You work, then you spend as fast as you're handed your pay, mostly you've spent in advance.'

Danny must have seen it was no use trying bravado.

'Someone stood the fare for me,' he mumbled.

'Why would they do that?'

'Because it was essential that I see you, Honor, ask you . . . beg you . . .'

'Beg me?' she queried.

'Yes—beg you. To beg you is why I'm here now. That was your second question. You asked me why?'

'And my third question, Danny?'

'You mean who told me where to come?'

'Yes.'

'The girls at your Sydney office wrote down the Odetta Hotel, Hong Kong.'

'But that's not *here*. Who told you *here*?'

'He did.'

'He?' she echoed.

'Chad's brother . . . at least a half-brother.'

'Like you are to me.'

'Honor——'

'I mean it,' said Honor hardly. 'And at times like this you don't even rate half with me, Danny. But who is Chad?'

'Chad is—well——'

'Danny, tell me at once. Who is he?'

'He's quite nice, really,' began Danny, but Honor broke in furiously.

'I remember you saying that once about someone whom, for certain urgent reasons of your own, you wanted me to marry,' she flung.

'Yes—yes, Honor.'

'And this Chad, is he—is he——'

'The same person, yes.'

There was a moment's silence in the room. From the top of the bench the kitchen clock ticked. It was the only noise.

'But, Honor, it's more urgent now, it's life or death,' Danny blurted.

'Oh, don't exaggerate, don't be melodramatic!'

'But it is, I tell you, to me prison would be death.'

'Prison?' Honor looked at him in complete surprise. 'What in heaven are you saying, you crazy boy, what scrape is it this time?'

'No scrape, also none of your misdemeanours, pranks or follies, nothing like that, Honor. Honor, I'm really deep into it this time. Right up to my neck.' Danny added wretchedly: 'My worthless neck.'

'Danny, what have you done?' she insisted.

'I didn't mean to, I swear I didn't.'

'You also didn't mean to run up bills, to smash a borrowed car, to do a dozen things.'

'I still swear I didn't mean this, and I

still don't know how it came about. Not really. Yet it must have been me. There was no one else.'

'Go on, Danny.'

'When it was pointed out to me, I was—shocked.'

'Pointed out by whom?'

'Chad.'

'The man you want me to——'

'Yes, Honor. He'd forget it then, it would never rear its head again.'

'You believe that?'

'I have to, I have nothing else.' Danny's voice was more a cry than an answer. 'Anyway, I'd believe Chad regardless. He's basically a decent sort. We've been friends. I like him and you would. Honor, I know you would.'

'Danny, be quiet, *be quiet!*' she exclaimed. 'I've never heard such a preposterous thing in all my life. You must be mad!'

'No, I'm frightened, frightened. The thing is too big for me this time, and I'm scared to death. Honor, you *have* to help.'

'I won't help. It's unthinkable. Why did you do it?' It was a redundant question, but still Honor asked it.

'Well, it wasn't for myself,' Danny mumbled, and in spite of her anger the simple reply tore at Honor's heart. For it was true that nothing Danny did was ever for himself. He was slipshod, he was careless, he was unthinking, but whatever badness he ever did was never born out of a wish for self-gain, but for a desire to help someone else. Probably it was because he was an inherent show-off, an egoist, a lover of limelight, but self-indulgence was never the root evil in Danny's case.

'As an accountant to your firm you "borrowed" some money, Danny, is that it?' she asked presently.

'Yes, it must be that.'

'Must have been?'

'Honor, I can't seem to think,' he muttered.

'You "borrowed" a sum of money intending to put it back later?'

'Yes.'

'But meanwhile you intended to multiply it to help others, make yourself the big, jolly fellow?'

'I suppose so—yes.'

'But whatever means you used—what means *did* you use, Danny?'

'Cards, I think.'

'You *think?*' she echoed.

'I'm not sure. I can't remember.'

'So it's cards you think?'

'Yes.'

'Cards that didn't turn up trumps for you. You lost.'

'Yes.'

'The loss was discovered by this man Chad?'

'Yes. He works with me. It's his elder brother's firm, as a matter of fact.'

'And this Chad . . . and this is the part I can't believe . . . said he'd fix things if you could fix a marriage?'

'Yes.'

'With me?'

'Yes.'

'Is that all?'

Wretchedly Danny blurted again: 'Yes.'

There was another silence. During the hollow quality of it Honor paced up and down the room.

'I can't believe you're serious, Danny, you've always been a difficult boy, but at least you've always loved me—or anyway, I thought you loved me.'

'I do, Honor, I always have, I always will, but it will be hard to do any loving of anybody locked away.' Danny's voice cracked.

'They wouldn't lock you away.'

'In a case like this they would.'

'A first offender?'

'But what an offence!'

There was a third silence, only the kitchen clock punctuating the void. The quiet seemed to go on into a small eternity.

Honor broke it unwillingly but knowing she had to. 'How much—was it?'

Danny mumbled a reply, mumbled it incoherently, but Honor still caught it. She caught, too, the back of a chair, caught it for support.

'That much?' she gasped. 'That much? Oh, Danny!'

Across the little kitchen they looked at each other . . . then looked away again.

## Chapter Four

It was four o'clock by the time Honor crept into bed.

Around three, Natalie had quietly come out, sized up their misery with a quick, intuitive glance, then put on a saucepan of milk to heat. The three of them had sat round the table with their hands cradling beakers of cocoa, and though Nat had offered no words of comfort, comfort had been there.

It was Nat who finally had bundled Danny out of the unit, descended the stairs with him and snared a taxi. Honor, knowing Danny, had a pretty good idea that it would be Nat, too, who would pay the taxi fare in advance.

When Nat had come back Honor had been rinsing the cups.

'To bed,' Nat had said firmly. 'You have to get up again in three hours.'

'I'm sorry you were disturbed, Natalie,' Honor apologised.

'It was nothing, I have all day to sleep, you have a business to go to.'

'All the same, you were imposed on, so you have a right to be told all about it. Do you want to hear the story?'

'Not at four in the morning. Heads down, Honor.' Nat herself had got into bed by now, so Honor had followed her example.

She had thought she would not sleep, she had thought the improbable—no, *impossible* things that Danny had told her would keep racing round her mind, disturbing her, tormenting her, but sleep she did, even to the extent of Nita coming in and shaking her awake.

'Rise and shine, working girl, we can't all be stand-down air hostesses.'

'No,' said Honor, coming alive painfully but hiding the pain, 'we can't. Thank you, Nita.' She hoped her hollowness did not show.

She made her coffee extra strong and put on her lipstick with a heavier hand. Then she went into the street, depending on people's interest in themselves and not her to get her through. She need not have worried, not in Hong Kong, where life, for all its apparent busyness, never got into its real stride until mid-morning. Nights were long nights, starting early, finishing late, and if the pace was obvious in the countenance of a fellow pedestrian, no one noticed, knowing they would be looking the same themselves.

No one at Bright Sun noticed, not even Mr Hing, but Kit, calling round at lunch as he always did now, noticed at once.

'If I hadn't left you last night cloistered in a safe and respectable unit I'd reckon you'd been on the spree, Honor. What gives?'

'Not on a spree and nothing gives,' sighed

Honor, then, because already Kit knew a lot of the story: 'Danny arrived.'

'At that time of evening!'

'Even later. We were in bed . . . at least nearly so.'

'And the wretch broke in?'

'He knocked on the door,' Honor corrected.

'So he *has* followed you over.'

'Yes.'

'But I thought you said he'd have no money.'

'He was loaned some,' she explained.

'Then he either must have a very good friend or a very good reason for coming, a very compelling reason.'

'Yes,' was all Honor could find in her to reply.

But it wasn't enough for Kit. He ignored her misery.

'Tell me all, darling, I want to know. After all, I have to, haven't I, for we're in everything now, together. What brought him here? How did he find the flat?'

'A very compelling reason, as you just said, brought Danny, Kit, and I'll say more about that later, but someone did tell him about the flat.'

'Who?'

'I don't know. Danny said "he", then he indicated that "he" was Chad's brother.'

'Chad?' he queried.

'The man who—who——'

'Say it, darling.'

'Who wants to marry me.' Honor bit her lip to stop herself from crying. 'Remember, Kit? I told you the ridiculous story before.'

There was a silence. For several moments Honor could not find the courage to look up at Kit, she was afraid of the anger that would be there; Kit certainly had been bitter the first time she had related it. Then she did look up . . . and was surprised. Far from being incensed this time Kit was— smiling.

'I always suspected I had good taste,' he was saying proudly, 'not only *I* fall for you but an unknown lover does as well. So much so that he even pays his dear love's brother to come and plead his cause.'

'Kit, don't speak like that,' she begged, 'it's distasteful.'

'But still a compliment, Honor, a compliment to you, so a compliment to me.'

'A compliment I don't want. I said no, of course.'

'Of course you did. Otherwise where would I be?' Kit gave his charming smile.

'The thing I can't understand,' fretted Honor, 'is why, *why* me?'

'Darling, don't be so humble, you're *lovely*. You're as beautiful a girl as I've seen.'

'I'm not, and even if I was there are lots of presentable girls.'

'My word was lovely, not presentable,' he corrected.

'Lots of them,' Honor repeated.

'Yet he still chose you.'

'. . . Yes.'

'Honor?' Kit had caught the note in Honor's voice.

'Yes, he chose me, Kit . . . but at a very high price.'

'What price?' Kit asked.

'The price—is Danny's freedom.'

'Freedom?'

'From prison, Kit.'

'Let me get this straight: Your brother is in trouble?'

'Grave trouble,' she sighed. 'It's the old, old story so far as I can follow. Danny is in the accountancy section of his firm. He works beside a junior member of the family who owns it. The young man he works beside is named Chad, and it's Chad who—who——'

'Fell in love with you?'

'Yes.'

'Well, what's wrong with that?'

'Nothing, I suppose . . . until it comes to blackmailing Danny.'

'With you as the price, the price of letting Danny off the hook?'

Again Honor said: 'Yes.'

Kit considered for a while, then asked: 'Danny helped himself illegally, I take it.'

'I expect so. He can't remember very well.'

'They never do. How much?'

In a shaken voice Honor told him and he gave a long low whistle.

'I can't believe it!'

'That's what Danny said,' she shrugged.

'He'd be put away for years.'

'Yes.'

'For an amount like that it's what he deserves.'

'I can't think he does deserve it, not really,' sighed Honor. 'He's terribly vague about it all, very uncertain.'

'They're all uncertain, it's part of the act.'

'Not Danny,' she insisted.

'Oh, come off it, pet, he's no different, except that that amount you tell me *is* different, it's sky-high. Why, the most ambitious thief in the world would be green with envy!'

'He's not a thief, Kit, I feel there's some awful mistake. For one thing a thief has to be avaricious, mercenary, and Danny never was. He never ever thought of himself.'

'Who else, then? And don't say sister Honor, when he would gladly use her as a bargaining point to go free.'

'It's not like that—it might look it, but it isn't. Not with Danny.'

Kit said wryly, 'It takes a lot of believing, my sweet.'

'But believe, *believe*, Kit.' Honor looked at him piteously.

'For you I would believe that black is white,' he said.

'Thank you,' Honor said tremulously as she mopped up a tear. 'I feel better now that you know.'

'Yet the position is still the same.' Kit paused. 'Unless——'

'Yes, Kit?'

'Unless you work on this Chad, plead Danny's cause.'

'At that price he has set?'

'You're right, he'd want more than a pretty face and a pleading voice.' Another pause. 'But there *is* something.'

'Yes?'

'You could marry me.'

'What, Kit?' she gasped.

'Marry me,' he repeated. 'I intended asking you sooner or later, so it may as well be sooner.'

'But how can that help? Danny then would be left entirely unprotected. He would be utterly dependent on the good will—or otherwise—of this Chad.'

'Yes, but Chad, once he saw marriage was too late, once he realised the uselessness of his demand, the nonevent of it all, might drop the matter. There's nothing more disheartening than a scheme that can't . . . not won't, Honor, but *can't* . . . come true. He could even forget the whole thing.'

'With that much money involved?'

'That is a problem, I agree, and I've no doubt it would have to be paid back over the years, but it's still an attempt.'

'Yes,' Honor said slowly. 'An attempt. But—marry you at once, Kit?'

He nodded. 'There's also another angle to it all. Us.'

'Us?' she queried.

'You and me. Us. Us. Us. When are we going to turn over this dismal page headlined Danny and start a page on Us? I love you—I loved you from the first moment I saw you. Marry me, Honor, and be strong in all this with my strength.'

Honor looked at him, looked at Kit, tall, young, handsome, upright, and suddenly wanted to lean, not have someone . . . *Danny* . . . lean on her.

'I do love you,' she said tremulously, 'but I think that even Hong Kong, that seems to have everything else, couldn't supply us with a marriage licence by this afternoon.'

'No, they couldn't do that, but why today?'

'Because Danny will be around again today.'

'Then at least we can be engaged. We'll buy the ring at once.'

'No, not good enough, Kit. An engagement ring promises but doesn't seal.'

'Then failing marriage, though believe me it won't be delayed one moment more than it has to be, why not—pretend?'

'Pretend?' she asked.

'A wedding ring is much cheaper than an engagement ring, my dear, and you don't have to produce a certificate unless you're asked. Would Danny ask?'

'N-no. But Danny would naturally know I wasn't married when he came last night.'

'Did you tell him you weren't?'

'We didn't talk about me, we talked about him—and other things.' Honor's face crumbled.

'Then he actually doesn't know?'

'No, but——'

'He doesn't know. We go on from there.'

'How can we? He still wouldn't believe it.'

'Not believe it, with Nita and Averil backing us up, saying they were witnesses? Oh, yes, they'll do that. They've seen me out of situations before.—No, none like this, sweet, but things I—well, I didn't want continued any more. They'd have to agree or I wouldn't play back with them.' Kit gave a low laugh. 'I'd never ask Nat,' he went on, 'but the girls——'

'I still don't see it solves anything,' sighed Honor.

'It solves it like this: *You can't marry the man your brother wants you to because you're already married,* and that is that. It's final. It's the end. It's amazing, Honor, how a positive answer can put a full stop to a thing.'

'And start a prison sentence for someone else?'

'Now that's very smart of you, sweet.'

Typical of Kit and his disregard of the public he kissed her.

'Show me that finger,' he demanded. 'Yes, I think I know the size. Go back to work now. Go home afterwards. I'll be round to stand by you, and together, Honor, we can beat the world.'

'Yes,' murmured Honor, trying to be reassured, 'we can beat the world.'

She went back to Bright Sun.

It was a miserable afternoon. The reassurance she had tried to achieve soon fell flat. She did not think Kit's subterfuge would work. It was only, as Kit had admitted, an attempt, but Danny needed more than an attempt, especially a fake attempt, for that after all was what they were doing, faking a marriage in the hope that it might release Danny. It was possible, very probable, that the subterfuge would be seen at once. The real thing would have been better. But . . . and Honor stood very still a moment, looking as though she was altering an arrangement in her mind but really facing up to a fact . . . did she want the real thing? That is—just yet? She loved Kit, she was sure of that, but she didn't want marriage under these circumstances. She wanted a bloom on things, and hurrying up a union just for convenience seemed to rub off the bloom somehow. Perhaps . . . pretending to dust an artifact . . . this 'fake' would be better after all.

Yet still unconvinced, still uncertain, she fretted all through the afternoon, then promptly at five o'clock she left.

She was glad that Kit was not outside Bright Sun waiting for her. He usually was, but he had said he would come to the flat later today.

'The "husband" must be brushed up and presentable,' he had smiled. 'Besides, I have to buy that ring.'

'How will I tell the girls?' Honor had asked.

'No hassle, I'll ring them myself. Don't anticipate trouble, darling, I can manage that pair.'

When Honor reached the unit she found that Kit had rung and that there was no trouble.

'We'll stick by you,' Nita breezed, 'that's what friends are for.'

'Especially Kit's friends.' If Averil's voice had a certain thin note it was barely perceptible.

'Why, we were even witnesses,' Nita went on.

Only Nat, standing silent at the door, did not laugh. When Honor looked a second time to the door Natalie had gone.

'Well,' the two girls demanded, 'aren't you going to get dressed up? After all, you don't get married all the time.'

'When—when was I married?' Honor asked uneasily.

'This afternoon,' Averil shrugged. 'The groom was so anxious he hasn't yet found a flat.'

'No, that won't do,' came in Nita, 'it's too recent, a marriage so recent could be nullified. No, Honor, you were married several days ago, and Kit is negotiating for a place. That could be true, there's quite a shortage of accommodation here.'

Honor stammered, a little embarrassed; 'It could still be nullified, couldn't it?'

'You mean *you* here, *Kit* over the harbour at Victoria?' It was still Nita. 'But, darling, that separation came *after* the honeymoon, a honeymoon in the Victoria Hilton, no less. Remember? Why, you even took the *Tak Fu* for a wedding treat. You book at the Hilton, so you'd be safe there.'

'*Tak Fu?* The pretty brigantine?'

'Meaning one million blessings.'

'One million,' remembered Honor, 'and one.'

'All very romantic,' came in Averil, and her voice still had that thin note. 'I should say that romance will save the day for you.'

. . . And save Danny? Honor winced.

She went in to change her dress. In spite of the warm evening her fingers were ice-cold as she fastened the buttons of her pink silk blouse. It was all only pretence, and a pretence with a cause, but she still didn't like it. She wanted Kit without pretence. In some way she could not have put words to, all this put a dullness to the gloss.

'Honor.' It was Kit at the door, a very handsome Kit in a new tropical suit, bought no doubt to make the bridegroom story sound even more true.

Honor went to him thankfully, and he held her a moment, then put a plain gold circle on her third finger.

'Mrs Blyth,' he sealed. They kissed.

Presently he whispered: 'Chin up, your "dear", and I mean that in another sense, brother has just arrived. With him is——' But Honor never heard the rest, she was going out to Danny.

Danny was waiting in the porch. The door to the outside hall had not been shut, rather as though there was someone else. Honor saw more than registered that.

'We'll talk in my room, Danny,' she said. 'We'll be alone there.' She gave Kit, who had followed her, a significant look.

Once in the room and the door closed, Honor asked banally: 'How do you feel?'

'How could I feel?' he groaned.

'Well, at least, Danny, you've had a night's sleep.'

'A long night on my back, you mean, because that was all it was. Still, I expect I must get used to staring into hopeless darkness night after night.'

'Danny darling, stop it, stop being defeated before you are,' she begged.

'Why? *Why*, Honor? Have you thought of something?' Danny's voice was pathetically eager. He looked almost achingly at her.

'No, darling, there's nothing to think, not really, and there's no way out—apart from miracles.'

'Which don't happen, not to me.—But Honor, what do you mean by "no way out"? There *is* a way. Remember? You.'

'I remember, but it's still No, Danny. It has to be.'

'Honor——' he begged.

'I told you so last night, but you wouldn't believe me, but you'll have to believe me now. You see—you see, I can't do it, Danny, not for you, not for anyone. Not when I'm already—married.'

Honor stepped closer to her brother and held out her hand with its golden circlet, and he stared back with dismay—and something else.

A deep hurt.

## Chapter Five

DEEP, deep hurt.

Honor knew it at once. Never before in her life had she kept anything away from Danny. From a little boy he had been as close to her and her thoughts as she was herself.

That was what he was remembering now, she read, and she saw the cloud hanging over him and hated herself for putting it there. She wanted to say: 'No, it's not true, dear, I'm only pretending, in a thing as big as marriage I would tell you first, of course.' But it was too late, she had started the lie, so she had to continue it.

'You've always confided things, Honor,'

Danny was saying painfully. 'I know I never deserved your secrets, but you still did. I just can't think that you haven't now.' He was turning away from her to hide his feelings, but she still saw that his eyes were bright with unshed tears. He had been like that as a very little child, Honor recalled, tearful but proudly never crying.

'You were pressing me, Danny,' she reminded him, 'pressing me unbearably.'

'Yes, I was. I was desperate, so I took it out on you. But Honor, and you must believe me, when it actually came to it I doubt if I could have kept on pressing you. I would have told Chad I'd go to prison instead. Oh, Honor, what a mess I'm in!'

What a mess we're both in, Honor thought inwardly, Danny facing what he faces, I acting a lie. I love Kit, but for all my love I'd sooner have a clear conscience as regards Danny. Perhaps Danny doesn't deserve my regrets, but he's still my brother . . . and he's Danny.

'Kit wondered,' she heard herself saying, 'if I might be able to prevail upon this Chad. Kit is my—husband, Danny, and I've told him everything.'

Danny appeared scarcely to hear her, he

seemed out of touch with everything but his own hurt.

'Danny, I must talk to the man who says you owe all this money. *Danny'* . . . as Danny still stood unheeding . . . *'I must talk at once.'*

She had raised her voice considerably, and the urgent note reached Danny.

'I'll call him,' he said hoarsely, and he went out to the porch.—So there had been someone with him, Honor registered dully. She watched Danny come back, then stand aside to let another figure pass through the door.

It was a young man whom Honor had never seen before, but, she thought wryly, she could have seen him anywhere. Fair hair. Silk shirt loose over grey slacks. Very scrubbed. Quite presentable, even moderately handsome. But that was all.

'This is Chad Evans,' Danny was mumbling. 'Chad, this is my sister Honor.'

'So you're Honor.' The man, older than Danny but not, judged Honor shrewdly, as old as she was, came forward and took her hand. He held it there.

It was the hand with the ring, and ironically she wondered how long it would take him to realise that. But he was either not

81

perceptive, or he was carried away with the moment, for all he did was hold her hand in his.

'This is scarcely the introduction I would have liked, Honor . . . may I call you Honor? you call me Chad . . . but circumstances have called the tune. It's not a nice tune, is it? But I believe Danny has already mentioned that.'

'Can I have facts, please, not tunes.' Honor heard her own voice, very cool, very clear, very crisp.

Chad Evans did not look pleased.

'Well, I don't know exactly how much Danny has told you,' he began, 'but if it's the stark truth you're after——'

'It is.'

'Then we, meaning the firm, are down in our balances, down very significantly, very disastrously.' He stopped and looked at Honor. 'Shall I go on?'

'Go on, please.'

'The discrepancies have all come from one source only. Need I still go on?'

'Yes.'

'Your brother's books,' Chad Evans complied in a low voice.

Before Honor could say anything he went on: 'Ordinarily there would be no way out for a large amount like this, not even for someone like Danny, whom I like very much. But as it happens there *could* be an escape, and I believe Danny has told you.'

'He has told me some ridiculous tale about marriage,' said Honor. '*Your* marriage with *me*.'

'You find it ridiculous?'

'And distasteful.'

He was silenced a moment, but he soon recovered.

'I see. Then it's no use my appealing that I'd fallen in love with you?'

'You hadn't even seen me!' she protested.

'I'd seen your photograph.'

'My——' Oh, Danny, Danny! Honor inwardly reproached.

Aloud she said: 'It would be no use at all.'

'Yet under the circumstances you'll still consider it?'

'Consider marriage with you?'

He nodded.

'No,' Honor said again.

'You mean you'd allow your brother to——'

'My answer is still no.'

'But why? Why? Admittedly you don't

know me, but surely the fact that I want to marry you——'

'Still no, Mr Evans,' she repeated.

'After all, it's a compliment.'

'No!'

'Also I'm not repulsive.'

'No, you're not repulsive,' she agreed, 'in fact you're good-looking, but——'

'Then is it the suddenness of it, the unusual aspects?'

'No.' Honor spoke quite calmly now, and she wondered at herself. 'It's really the fact that I can't have two husbands at the same time. It's really the fact that I'm married already.' As she had with Danny, she extended her hand with its plain gold ring.

A moment went by in stunned silence. Then Chad Evans turned quite savagely on Danny.

'You knew this all along!' he snarled.

'I didn't, Chad.'

'You were playing for time.'

'No, Chad!'

'Then you must have told her . . . told your sister last night.'

'I told her a month ago. You instructed me to prepare the way.'

'But you told her definitely last night, not merely prepared the way. I knew I should have come, too, not left you on your own. You admitted to her what you had done and at what price you could get out of it.'

'Yes, I did that.'

'With the result that she went off and—and——'

'Yes.' It was Honor, still cool and collected. 'She did. And now this unbelievable, quite unthinkable, abominable business is over.' She closed her lips and looked challengingly at Chad.

He must have seen her finality, for he grew sulky and hostile, and Honor realised too late that she was not going about things in the way Kit had advised.

'A ring doesn't make a marriage,' he snapped angrily.

Honor took a risk and asked: 'Do you want to see my certificate, then?'

Her frankness must have jerked him into acceptance, for he replied at once: 'No . . . no, of course not.'

'But perhaps you'd like some details. We were not married, as you're evidently thinking, on the spur of the moment, we were married several days ago. The two girls here were witnesses. You can call them in if you like, hear what they have to say.

Because there's a housing shortage my husband and I still stayed in our units while Kit tried to find a flat. But' . . . hurriedly and hotly . . . 'we did honeymoon in the Hilton in Victoria, and' . . . getting reckless now . . . 'we even took an evening cruise on the *Tak Fu*, which means, in case you don't know, One Million Blessings. We felt they were our blessings. Now are you satisfied?'

'That someone has beaten me to it? Yes, I suppose I have to be. But I'm not satisfied about the deficit I shall have to report . . . and I don't think your brother is satisfied with what it will mean to him.'

There was a hollow silence for a long moment.

Honor broke it. 'Perhaps we could come to some arrangement,' she said nervously, 'make amends over a period of time.' She looked around rather hopelessly. She knew she could never raise the amount, and she knew that Kit wouldn't even if he could.

'That would scarcely satisfy our shareholders,' Chad replied.

There was another hollow pause. Again Honor broke it. She asked Chad curiously: 'What makes me important enough to wipe out a debt?'

86

'You mean you will?' Chad said eagerly.

'No, I won't, but I'd still like to know.'

'I told you—I fell in love with the picture Danny showed me.'

'. . . And something else?'

'You're a bright girl. Yes. I knew with you I could win Aunt Lucia.'

'Aunt Lucia?' she queried.

'An old rich relation who's been rather parsimonious with her hand-outs lately. The most recent cheque I even felt like posting back . . . except that it came with advice.'

'Advice?' queried Honor.

'That if I were to settle down with a nice girl things might be different.'

'But why me?' she persisted.

'Because your photo *was* nice . . . nice enough, I saw at once, even for Aunt Lucia.'

'So there was no love,' Honor said derisively.

'I could have loved you for ever,' Chad assured her drily.

Again they relapsed into silence. Then Danny spoke.

'Could Honor *pretend* she was married to you?' He said it rather futilely, as though it was expected of him to say something and this was all he could think.

Chad Evans had narrowed his eyes on Danny. He moistened his lips.

'No wonder I always liked you, young Dan,' he said presently. 'You're hopeless, but you do bring a ray of hope.'

'You mean——'

'I mean it could be done . . . that is if the lady agrees.'

'Pretend I was married to you?' Honor said scornfully.

'Yes, Honor,' Danny came in, 'pretence. You know what's meant by pretence.'

'Yes.' For the briefest of moments Honor looked down at her hand. 'I know pretence, but——'

Chad had stepped forward. He was smiling again.

'I'll tell you *all* the story, not just loose bits.'

Before Honor could answer Chad was speaking eloquently about his aged aunt. He made quite a sentimental version of it. He spoke at length of his aunt's . . . great-aunt, actually . . . preference for him in the family. He described his deep devotion to her. He said how before she died he wanted her to see the girl he had married, especially since he had sent her Honor's picture. Honor looked at Danny and Danny looked away.

'It would be entirely for my aunt, not for myself,' Chad told Honor.

'You mean you would have no inheritance in view?' Honor had an edge to her voice.

Diplomatically he passed that over.

'Forget me,' he suggested, 'concentrate on your brother instead. Everything done would be done for him. Then what, seeing you don't have to go through a ceremony with someone obviously distasteful to you, could you lose?'

'I would lose by acting a lie.' (But, thought Honor, I'm already doing that with Kit.)

'A loss,' he agreed, 'but nothing really wrong, really bad.'

'I'm afraid I don't see it like that. I don't like deceit.' (Yet I'm deceiving of my own accord, she thought.)

'Then I'm sorry, too, sorry for Aunt Lucia, for myself . . . but most of all for Danny,' Chad said deliberately and a little brutally.

There was another silence, more hopeless than before. They were getting nowhere.

Beyond the balcony of the unit which faced Hong Kong harbour Honor could see the lights of a boat crossing from Victoria to Kowloon. It could be the *Tak Fu*, she thought, on its evening journey, *Tak Fu* meaning One Million Blessings.—Was there any blessing left anywhere just now? Any blessing for Danny?

There was still a blessing left for her, thank heaven, there was Kit, dear Kit, Kit who would never agree to any of this.

She said proudly and without hesitation this time: 'Kit, my husband, would never hear of such a thing.'

'No?' asked Chad. 'He has no interest in money?'

'Money?'

'He would not be asked to keep quiet without being "thanked", of course.'

'He wouldn't be interested in money, that kind of money.'

'Or all kinds of money?' Chad inferred. 'Nor,' he went on cruelly, 'in the money his brother-in-law cannot satisfactorily explain, how will he feel about that?'

'As badly as I do, no doubt, but he would still not want me to do what you say. He would be aghast.'

'. . . But even more aghast at now being closely related to a—I'll leave it at that because it hasn't a pretty sound.' Chad gave a low laugh.

'No. No, not quite like that.' There was

a voice at the door and the three of them wheeled around.

Hugh Rowan stood there.

The two boys were completely surprised, but their reaction was nothing to Honor's. She stood astounded and incredulous. Where did Hugh Rowan fit in?

'I think we all have a lot to discuss.' His voice came with a cutting quality, it seemed to whip around them. 'But not here, not in this lady's room.' He nodded at Honor. 'We'll move round to the hotel. Chad, you get going. Take this fellow with you.' This was Danny. 'Take Blyth who's waiting outside.'—Why Kit? Honor asked mutely. 'Take the girl, take Natalie.'

'Why Natalie?' This time Honor did break in.

Hugh Rowan turned and looked coldly at Honor. 'I could say propriety, four men and one woman, but I doubt, miss . . . no, madam now, isn't it . . . if you would understand the word. Actually the reason is that I don't expect a pleasant interlude, and in all fairness the lady should have some support in the presence of someone her own sex.

'But before we leave I wish to speak personally to Mrs Blyth, Chad.' He turned to Honor. 'I believe that was the name.' He turned back to Chad. 'All right, do as I say.'

'Yes, Hugh.'

'When you get to the hotel ring for some refreshments to be sent up to my suite. After that, wait. Is that clear?'

'Yes, Hugh, clear.'

Without another word Chad and Danny left the room; after some quiet discussion outside, this time with added voices, Kit's and Nat's voices, they left the flat.

Either Nita and Averil had gone out or gone to bed, for the unit lay dark and silent.

Across her and Nat's small space Honor looked at Hugh Rowan, then, unable to meet his cold glance any longer, she looked to the floor instead. Looked, though she would never have admitted it to him, with shame, shame over a small gold circlet now searing her finger and seeming to burn: 'Cheat!'

The ring was the first thing Hugh Rowan spoke about. He crossed and took up Honor's hand, then drawled: 'Even the fusing is still warm. How long have you had it? Ten minutes?'

'No.'

'Less?'

'Don't be absurd!' she snapped.

'Don't *you* be absurd,' he retorted, 'thinking you can put over a thing like that.'

'I'm not putting anything over. I am married. Do you want proof?' She had tried it successfully with Chad, boldly now she tried it with Hugh Rowan.

To her dismay he answered: 'Yes.' Then at once, and to her relief: 'No. No, it would only be a furthering of the lie, wouldn't it? However, I'm not blaming you, not entirely. I couldn't blame anyone not wanting to marry Chad.'

'Then why are you making this fuss?'

'It could be that I do blame anyone marrying that other fellow.'

'Other fellow?' she queried.

'Young Blyth.'

'Kit.'

'Yes.'

'Kit is *my* fellow, as you put it.'

'I do put it,' he said, 'and I could put out a lot more expressions regarding your so-called choice.'

'Not so-called,' she protested.

'Except' . . . he ignored her . . . 'that I still don't believe it.'

'Believe what?'

'You.' He took her hand again, this time quite roughly. 'This.'

'Then why don't you? Have—have you been talking to Kit?' Surely Kit had not told him the truth?

He was watching her face, and his smile was thin.

'Yes. But he didn't come clean, so don't worry.'

'Not even after you bullied and badgered him, because that would be your threatening form.'

'What had I to threaten with? Not gaol, as Chad had with your brother. Oh, no, only being deprived of his—wife, which couldn't be deprivation, could it, because he never had her as his wife.'

'We were married,' she insisted.

'When?'

'Long enough to—'

'Go on.'

'You're hateful!' she snapped.

'Go on,' he repeated.

'Then long enough to seal it.' Her cheeks were now flag-red, but her chin was up.

Hugh Rowan stood regarding her a long uncomfortable moment. 'You don't make a good liar,' he said.

'Because I'm telling the truth.'

'All right, we'll leave it like that at the moment, we'll say that the lady is telling the truth.'

'But it's not for you to say, is it? All this has nothing to do with you.'

'It's everything to do with me, you little fool,' he gritted. 'Do you think I'm here for the company? for the fun? If so, let me tell you if I had my way I wouldn't be within miles of this place, within miles of my brother, your brother, your—husband, most of all of you.'

'There's nothing to stop you putting those miles between us now,' Honor pointed out coldly.

'Oh, yes, there is. There's Aunt Lucia, who happens to be my aunt, too, and whom I happen to love—love, a word of four letters you know nothing about, not even' . . . coming a step closer to her . . . 'as a loving wife.' He waited a moment.

'Now,' he said, 'we will join the conference at the hotel and see what can be salvaged in the way of sanity' . . . a pause . . . 'and self-respect?'

He stood back and bowed her out, and Honor, confused and bewildered, obeyed. She went silently down the stairs beside him, silently down the street.

Once outside the building he told her they would walk.

'At this time of night it's hard to get a taxi, and it's only several streets.'

Then he began saying things, things that seared into Honor. He had been told about Miss Honor Jason when he was recently in Sydney, he said tersely. His half-brother had shown him her photo, told him they were going to be married.

'But——' endeavoured Honor, only to be rudely ignored.

'Chad was really excited about the girl,' went on Hugh Rowan, 'he was absolutely confident that our Aunt Lucia would be very happy with her sweetness (or so it appeared in the picture) as well. He said the two of them would visit Aunt Lucia.'

'You believed all that!' Honor was incredulous.

'Naturally I didn't know what "all that" entailed . . . not then. But I found Chad agreeably expansive for once, something he'd never been with me before in all his life. Aunt Lucia, old, frail, obviously at the end of her days, also influenced me. I wanted her contentment. So' . . . a shrug . . . 'I duly gave my blessing.'

'Not one million blessings?' Honor inserted a little hysterically.

'Nor one million and one,' he came back.

'I returned here,' he went on, 'quite looking forward to meeting Chad's girl when she arrived.—Then by chance I heard her name spoken. I saw her in the company, the close company, of someone else.'

'Girl meets boys,' Honor murmured, enlightened now.

Once more he shrugged.

'Chad duly arrived, and with him your own half-brother. Quite a coincidence, isn't it? Two half-brothers.' He gave a thin smile. 'The pair were naturally upset not to find you waiting at the hotel.'

'There was no such pre-arrangement,' she assured him.

'No? Yet they contacted me at once.'

'So you came to their rescue, having found out previously where I was.'

'Can you blame me? I was only thinking of Aunt Lucia . . . whom, incidentally, it appears now that *you* were only thinking about as well.'

'What do you mean, Mr Rowan?'

'Aunt Lucia was the sole reason you accepted Chad.'

'I never accepted him,' she contradicted. 'I never even saw your brother.'

'You accepted him,' persisted Hugh Rowan, 'because he was the only way out, through Aunt Lucia's expected benevolence, for your own brother. It was all done entirely for money, escape money. I didn't know that when I blamed you for having other strings to your bow that day, but I do know now.'

'That's why you called me naïve later at the Bright Sun when we talked about your aunt's island?'

'After you expressed a lack of knowledge of it, yes.'

'Apart from Mr Hing in casual conversation, and then from you, I'd never heard of your aunt or the island,' she told him.

'More pretence.' Another narrow smile.

They walked on in silence for a while. Honor broke it tremulously.

'If you know all these things,' she said, 'you also know Danny's troubles.'

'I didn't at first. I do now.'

'And you think that I——'

'What else is there to think? You are here, aren't you?'

'By chance only.'

'You expect me to believe that?' he ground out.

'I expect nothing from you. I came here because I could no longer put up with what Danny was begging of me. I would have gone anywhere, any place, but I had a job waiting in Hong Kong, so——' Honor spread her hands. She looked at Hugh Rowan desperately, had he only looked down. He didn't. He kept walking, so Honor walked, too.

'Meanwhile,' Hugh Rowan said, 'you got cold feet about Chad, even though he meant an escape for your brother. So you cunningly invested in a ring and a lie.'

'I did not!'

'Then your boy-friend did.'

'I married Kit,' she insisted.

He hunched his shoulders, but this time did not comment.

She waited for him to go on.

'But all was not lost,' he said presently, and his voice was thin, 'for you and Chad promptly instigated a new game and it was not the truth game. You were to "pretend" to poor Aunt Lucia that you and my brother were the blissful couple she naturally wanted you to be, at the same time make Chad the triumphant legatee he so wanted to be, as well as let Danny off the hook—and all, mark you, at no matrimonial inconvenience to yourself. In other words, you would have your cake and eat it. When I overheard all this just now, miss . . . madam . . . I was sickened. But have no fears, at this point of time I will not be contending anything. I have my reasons.'

'Reasons?' she repeated.

'No more words, now, please. We've arrived.'

He led her through the large swinging doors of the Hotel Odetta. Together they crossed the reception hall to the lifts.

## Chapter Six

THE lift went silently up to the penthouse floor. As the door slid smoothly open Honor saw *all* Hong Kong, not merely a sliver of it as she had been allotted in her lower Odetta room, unrolled before her. The effect was quite stunning. She had never looked on such brilliance, such glitter in her life, and for a heady moment, swaying slightly with the shimmering magnificence of it, she instinctively reached out and held on to her companion's arm to steady herself.

'Yes, it grabs you like that,' Hugh Rowan said, for the first time in a long while losing his edged bitterness, and he stopped and supported her instead.

'I'm sorry.' Honor stepped away at once.

'For what? Never apologise for beauty, for it is very beautiful, isn't it, man-made notwithstanding.'

'The water isn't man-made,' she commented.

'True, and in this instance man is augmenting nature with his ships and lights. It makes for a wonderful partnership, something I believe in very much.' He paused. 'Do you?'

'Wonderful partnerships?'

'Yes.'

'So we're going to start all *that* again!'

He looked at her a long time, and if Honor had looked back at him, with a certain disappointment. 'We are on opposed roads,' he said. The hardness came back to his voice again. 'Eventually,' he went on, 'we're going to start much more than *that*. But not at once. The others haven't heard us arrive' . . . he nodded to the closed doors . . . 'so let's forget things for a moment and drink it all in.' He barely touched her elbow with his cool fingers to lead her to the parapet.

'Before we enter the horror chamber,' he suggested, 'look round. Do you know anything of Hong Kong yet?'

'You should be able to answer that yourself. I didn't know the way from the Bright Sun to the harbour, remember?'

'But that was some time ago, and you are, I think, a quick worker.'

'Is that another of your barbed questions?' she snapped.

'Surely you don't object to being labelled smart?'

'At what?' Honor flashed.

'Your work?' he said blandly. 'Mr Hing is very enthusiastic about your work. Perhaps your ease of acclimatisation? Natalie tells me you've settled down in this city quite creditably.—Or your adroitness in marriage?'

'Ah, I was waiting for that!'

'Then I'm glad I haven't disappointed you,' he drawled.

A fuming moment went past for Honor.

'Why have you been checking up on me like this?' she asked.

'I haven't. Mr Hing volunteered his section of my information. We're old friends,

Mr Hing and I, and as I'm an Australian he naturally thought I would like to hear all about a fellow Australian.'

'But you're not an old friend of Natalie's, and you evidently checked there,' Honor pointed out.

'I think most people would be old friends of Natalie's in a very short time.'

Honor had nothing to say to that, and he used her silence to return to the subject of Hong Kong.

'It was Chinese once, you would know that, and physically and geographically, in fact in every way except politically, it's still Chinese. The British landed in the last century . . . Hong Kong was only a place of fishermen and pirates then . . . and, in spite of being prohibited from Cantonese waters, they stayed on. From such small beginnings an immense and glorious city and a superb and beautiful harbour have evolved.' Hugh Rowan held out his arms to the spectacle beneath them.

'The credit would be to the Chinese as well as the British,' Honor said. 'They're a kindly people.'

'Of course. Where else would a family of five or six live year after year in the confines of a fishing boat about the size of a small bungalow entrance hall? You've seen these junks?'

'Yes.'

'But the Chinese, too, are adaptable. They can live both ways. You'll be aware of this when we take tea at the Hings'.'

'We?' she queried.

'You and I.'

'But——' she began.

'I'm sorry, your husband was not invited. I don't think Mr Hing knows you've married.'

'Then "we" means—us?'

'Yes.'

'You said adaptable in both ways,' she reminded him.

'Mr Hing lives in a mansion.'

'And he has asked—us for tea?'

'For you to meet the five daughters. Already, I think, you've met Madam Hing.'

'She came to Sydney with Mr Hing,' Honor told him.

'You'll fall in love with the girls. I have already. But you don't look enthusiastic,' he went on. 'Don't tell me it's jealousy? If so, I haste to reassure you that they're of tender years.'

'I wasn't looking jealous, I was looking

surprised. I thought a period of displeasure faced me, not pleasure.'

'All work and no play makes for dull results. There *is* to be a settling up eventually, have no two thoughts about that, but not at once, not for another week, anyway. I'm obliged to remain here in Kowloon on business for another week. Besides, the weather——'

'The weather?'

He gnawed at his lip with strong white teeth as though annoyed with himself about something.

'After that,' he went on very quickly, 'we shall see.'

'See what?'

'Lee Fin, of course.'

'Lee Fin?' queried Honor.

'My—our aunt's island.'

'An English-owned island in Hong Kong!'

'Yes. It all happened a long time ago. Possession laws no doubt would be very different today.'

'But it is privately owned?'

'Yes. See what you missed when you became ordinary Mrs Blyth. You could have been the princess presumptive of Lee Fin instead of Mrs Blyth of Suburbia.'

'I would sooner be what I am,' Honor assured him.

'Which is?' He waited.

After a moment he said: 'Come. We've already kept these people apprehensive far too long.'

Without another word Hugh Rowan crossed to the penthouse and swung open the door for Honor to enter. After she had walked unwillingly in, he came in as well, shutting the door behind them, pulling several blinds.

'We are not here,' were his first terse words, 'to enjoy the view.' His reproof included everybody.

He nodded Honor to a chair and took one himself.

It was a substantial suite; Honor could see a number of smaller rooms leading from this largest room, but she also noted that none of the group had left to take cover in some corner. Instead they waited docilely at the table for the judge to begin his inquest. To Honor it seemed like that.

On the table were the refreshments that Chad had been directed to order. There was champagne in a bucket, silver salvers of sandwiches, cups to accompany a long pot of coffee. At an indicative nod from the leader, Honor took up the coffee, which everyone at once preferred.

'You ordered wrongly, Chad,' Hugh Rowan drawled. 'This is not a celebration, it's an investigation. Thank you' . . . to Honor as she passed him a cup . . . 'perhaps we shall come to the other later.'

Honor very much doubted this. Her first look, when she had entered, had been to Danny. He was seated beside Natalie, for which Honor was grateful, but he was obviously very down in spirits. Kit, the subject of her second glance, was little brighter, and the same with Chad. No, there would be no celebrating here.

Someone passed sandwiches, which were barely tasted, then Hugh Rowan pushed aside his cup and said:

'Now we will face facts. The first and most contributing fact is a discrepancy in some accounts.' He was looking directly at Danny. 'You deny or admit this?'

'I admit it, but I swear I never intended——'

Danny was stopped by Hugh Rowan's big upheld hand.

'It never is intended,' he said drily.

'Next we come to my brother Chad, who had the brilliant idea of covering up for his friend—but at a price. It seems' . . . still dry . . . 'we all have a price.'

'Even you?' Honor heard herself insert.

'Yes.' Hugh Rowan answered her at once, but he did not look at her. He went on with the ritual.

'My brother Chad had previously fallen in love' . . . a long pause . . . 'with this lady on the right of me—well, either that or he fell in love with the possibility of what such a love could assure.'

'Really, Hugh!' Chad put in, but his brother only shrugged.

'I'm not going through all this to make any of you wretched,' he said to the assembly, 'I'm really endeavouring to explain to Natalie, who happens to be the one innocent party here, and who must be wondering what it is all about.'

'No, I know,' Natalie said in her quiet voice. 'Danny told me.'

'Told you everything?'

'All he knew.'

'Which was *not* all, as we now are aware. For instance, he didn't know that his sister, whom Chad, through him, had planned to marry, had so disliked the idea that she had gone and married someone else, thus leaving *nobody* for Chad's schemes, *nobody* for the distraught brother to turn to, *no way out* for any one, unless' . . . a brief thin smile . . . 'she agreed to a game called Pretence.'

'Which' . . . it was Honor now and in as cool a voice as Hugh Rowan's . . . 'I have not.' She became sharply aware that everyone round the table was looking at her.— That Kit was looking. Without looking back at him she still had the sensation of stunned dismay in him. Why was Kit looking like that?

Hugh Rowan broke the ensuing silence. He addressed himself ostensibly to Natalie again.

'At no time was I completely easy about any of this; I was dubious over Chad's initial statement that he was going to marry a Miss Jason and take her to meet Aunt Lucia. I thought it could have another side to it . . . and I know now it did. But I couldn't know then, and loving my aunt I only thought of her, even though I couldn't see how such a girl, or so the lady seemed in the photograph I was shown, could possibly be coupled with Chad. Yes, Chad, I'm saying that. As it has turned out, she was not, though' . . . a shrug . . . 'until I knew that——'

'It was a case of girl meets boys when

109

Mr Rowan met me,' Honor came in frivolously, not caring whether the others understood. 'Well' . . . boldly . . . 'why not? This boy was Kit, and I was attracted to Kit.' She looked proudly around the table. 'So much so,' she finished challengingly, 'that we were married.'

No one spoke.

'So,' went on Hugh Rowan after a few moments, 'a comedy of errors was staged . . . except it's *no* comedy, particularly to two people. To my aunt. To this young man.' He looked at Danny. 'That's why an alternative to marriage is being suggested, in short a *pretence* of marriage. In spite of her marital state Miss—no, Mrs Blyth—is being asked to *pretend* she married my brother, thus helping an old lady die happy and at the same time saving her own brother from arrest. For it would have to be arrest. Chad might be quiet, I might be, but you could never quieten a team of shareholders.'

'But how could you if I pretended marriage?' Honor asked curiously.

'Very simply. Our Aunt Lucia, overjoyed, would undoubtedly advance Chad a substantial sum of money.—Or that is what's hoped, I believe?' Hugh looked to Chad.

'I'm certain she would,' Chad broke

in eagerly, 'and with it I would vindicate Danny.' He looked at Honor, Danny did the same, Hugh Rowan, Natalie, but Kit—Honor saw Kit avert his head.

'Kit,' she called down the length of the table. 'Kit, it's your turn to speak.'

But Kit only kept looking away, and a silence enveloped the room. Though not entirely silent. Because she was sitting beside him Honor alone heard the low: '. . . we all have our price' of Hugh Rowan's. Her fingers cut into the palms of her hands. Kit couldn't . . . Kit wouldn't . . . not Kit!

'So now we sum things up,' Hugh Rowan said smoothly. 'To prevent this young man paying a harsh debt to society, as it's ironically put, to be kind to an old lady, we now ask Mrs Blyth will she forgo that "Mrs Blyth" and be briefly Mrs Evans instead. It will be entirely false, of course, but something, I think, not entirely foreign to Mrs Evans?' He looked down at Honor.

Honor, still sitting stunned, sat up. 'Why should you think that?'

'Because we're all practised in pretence.'

'You, too?'

'I, too.'

'Why does there have to be a pretence?'

she demanded. 'You're a rich man, you could free Danny.'

'I have no reason to, Chad has . . . or he had. The reason was you. Anyway'. . . a bland smile . . . 'the masquerade would be brief, perhaps only a bedside appearance. Then after it's done, the bride . . . Mr Blyth's bride, not Chad's . . . would be free to go back to her rightful husband, her brother, with his debt paid up through Chad, would be free to begin again. So what do you say, Mrs Blyth?' Mocking eyes were turned on Honor.

'I don't want to say anything. I want to think . . . take time.'

'Which you shall have. As I told you before, I can't get over to the island before a week. I have business here.'

'I could go, Hugh,' broke in Chad eagerly. 'I could take Honor with me.'

'I doubt if she would go with you even if I allowed it, and I don't intend to allow it. No, a week from today we'll all cross to Lee Fin on my boat.—Mrs Blyth, of course, first agreeing.' Again the blue mocking look.

'All of us?' someone asked.

'All. The pretence bride and groom, naturally. The bride's brother, who might have ideas of getting away if we didn't keep him under surveillance.'

'No, I wouldn't leave,' Danny protested, but Hugh Rowan ignored him.

'Mrs Blyth's legitimate husband most assuredly, for he couldn't be expected to stay away from his wife. Natalie' . . . a smile at the girl . . . 'because one woman to four men would not be fair on Mrs Blyth. Myself.'

'All packaged up.' Honor's voice was frozen.

'Not quite. It needs the string around it. You.

'No!' Again Honor looked down the table, looked first at Chad's anxious face, then at Danny's distressed one. Lastly she looked at Kit. Kit, Kit, she cried inwardly, stand up and protest, say that—say——

But Kit sat on.

'You have time yet, Mrs Blyth.' It was Hugh Rowan again. 'Through the week I'll contact you and you will let me know your decision. Now, having done the investigations, shall we start on the celebrations?'

'Celebrations?' asked Honor dully.

'Celebrating the fact that now, if nothing else, we understand each other a little better. For we do, don't we?' He gave her a quick flint look. 'Open the bottle, Chad.'

His brother did, and the glasses were filled.

'To still better understanding,' Hugh Rowan toasted, and he held his glass aloft.

Honor shut her eyes and drank.

She did not see Kit again that night. She and Nat were whisked down the lift, put into a taxi and returned to the unit before Honor quite realised what was happening.

Nat went to bed at once, not lying in the dark and exchanging confidences with Honor as they had come to do and look forward to. She was asleep when Honor left in the morning.

Mr Hing came up to the display during the day, expressing delight that Miss Jason and Mr Rowan would be taking tea at his home during the week. Honor bowed in the way she had unconsciously slipped into since coming to Hong Kong and insisted that it was their, her and Mr Rowan's, pleasure.

Kit did not turn up at lunch, and after waiting again when she left work with the same result, Honor took the street down to the harbour, a direct way that she knew very well now, and a way that usually caused a smile as she recalled what an arduous journey she had previously made of it. But there was no smile in her today. Her mind was on Kit, and it was an uneasy mind.

But the harbour proved a solace. Today it wore its turquoise dress. Yesterday it had been jade green. It was difficult to say which dress she preferred. Small boys were flying kites in an adjacent park, dodging between the ever-present exercisers with their flexing and bending, and as the little kite manipulators were expert at their job, the blue air above was full of weaving patterns. On the ground and on the water the usual busyness prevailed, pedlars calling and extolling their wares as they walked along the crowded streets or hopped between junks and sampans. Never once did the incredible number of boat craft collide, and Honor felt sure you could have examined each hull and not found a scratch.

Kit found her there later, caught up in the thrall of waterside Hong Kong, and that was why, Honor thought a little wryly, her welcome was not what she had planned. She had been confused and hurt by Kit's behaviour last night, and she had not intended to greet him eagerly. But eagerness *was* Hong Kong, she thought resignedly as she went to his arms.

'Darling, I thought you'd walked out on me!' Kit said reproachfully.

'You weren't there,' she pointed out.

'No, I met this old friend.'

'It was an old friend last time,' Honor said drily.

'Honor, don't let's waste time examining, let's just be.'

'It doesn't seem you want to "just be", not after your silence last night.'

'Not forbidding my "wife" to be part and parcel of that stunt, you mean?'

'Yes.'

'So it's to be a post-mortem after all,' he commented.

'No, it's not, Kit, but I feel you should tell me why you didn't back me up when I was so—well, indecisive.'

'Because, darling, I knew you were not indecisive, not really, because I knew you had no other choice.'

'You mean Danny?'

'Naturally.'

'. . . Kit, would it matter so much to you if Danny was——'

'Arrested? Well, I wouldn't like it. But

116

much more to the point, I knew how it would matter to you.'

'And that was the only reason you kept silent?' In spite of herself Honor could not help thinking of a soft voice beside her intoning '. . . we all have our price.' But of course Kit had only kept quiet because of her.

'What other, darling?' Kit said, hurt.

'I suppose you're right . . . but would a— husband have complied so easily?'

'But I'm not. Remember?' Kit was grinning now.

'No, we're not married. Then would a— lover?' Honor was not smiling.

'Darling, don't say that,' he begged.

'Say what?'

'That I'm not your love. Honor, look at me, my sweet.'

Honor did, and it was impossible to resist him. From the first moment she had sat beside him on the plane she had felt herself reacting to him, reaching out to him, and now she did again.

'But, Kit,' she reproached, 'if only you'd objected——'

'Believe me I did, Honor, in my heart.'

'Your heart?'

'My heart, sweet, now your heart as well.

Look, dear, in a week, less, it will all be over. We'll cross to this island as arranged, Chad will say his piece to his aunt, then produce you, then we all can come back. Danny can begin life again. *We* can begin.'

He was irresistible when he was like this, the brilliant sun in his hair turning the ends to gold, his eyes begging her.

'It was only you I was thinking of, Honor. It's always only you.' In typical Kit fashion he ignored the passing parade . . . most of them Cantonese and traditionally disapproving of any public emotion . . . and he kissed her.

The kiss still held the first thrill, and after the briefest of hesitations, Honor kissed him back.

## Chapter Seven

WOMANLIKE, Honor began to worry about dress, or rather what one wore when one took tea with a family like the Hings. She could definitely not see herself in denim, not beside formally-suited Mr Hing, elegantly-gowned Mrs Hing, or the five little girls whom she had not met but who Hugh Rowan had said were charming.

Here in Hong Kong anything went for a Westerner, be it dresses, top and skirts (either middy or mini), slacks . . . even shorts. Also nowadays anything went, very often, for a local girl. The times of kimonos and cheongsams were over in the capital; they were worn only by hostesses or guides. Out in the rural towns they could still be seen upon occasion, but mostly the country mompes or black trousers were favoured, and not always the traditional frogged tunics with them, either. Honor had seen quite a few nylon blouses, and once even a T-shirt.

She thought about asking Hugh Rowan, but decided proudly not to. She could not ask Natalie, for Nat had left the day after the Odetta conference for her Philippines hostess stint, left quite eagerly since it meant she would be back again for the trip across to Lee Fin. She seemed to be looking forward to that, and, as far as Honor could judge, none of them was averse to it . . . except herself.

'Little use my being averse,' Kit had grimaced when she had remarked on this, 'Rowan knows my department boss, and I've been given the time off whether I want it, or not. You've no idea, Honor, how many people that fellow knows, and the strings he can pull.'

Returning later to the vexatious subject of clothes, Honor still had wondered *what*. Though trousers were worn more often than skirts by the Cantonese women, she felt it might be different for her for a tea occasion. For one thing, to wear trousers like the Cantonese did you needed Cantonese hips, something Westerners did not have. That settled one thing, then, it would be a skirt. But what material? How long? What colour?

White, which had once been reserved for mourning, Honor had learned, was more prevalent now, but mostly worn by school-girls, so white was out. Red was the country's colour, and nationally favoured, so Honor ruled that out, too, as being the people's privilege. She ruled with it the near-pinks and roses, and found herself then with a simple yellow, green or blue choice. Mr Hing had called her a sprig of wattle, so perhaps she had better not wear yellow. Green, perhaps? Blue? Yes, blue.

There were plenty of places at which to choose a dress, the best of the world's couturiers were represented here, and at a far lower price than in the country where they made their creations. Also dressmakers abounded. They attended every visiting ship, took measurements and produced a dress in a day. Also, a perfect fit, for Hong Kong was known for fit.

Nevertheless Honor did not take a risk of not liking the finished article when she got it, and instead walked up and down the dressmaking and high fashion area until she saw a French model that seemed it. It was expensive, but how much more expensive would it have been in Paris? Anyway, and Honor could not have said why, she simply had to have it. She had to look right for the Hings . . . and for *him*. Well, at least she had to show him!

She went in, tried on the dress, touched the smooth jersey of it, felt pleasure at the dreamy forget-me-not hue of it, then came out with a smart box that she hid among her display articles so as not to hurt Mr Hing. The Bright Sun, being an emporium, had racks of dresses, but somehow it did not seem right to buy one to wear to your employer's house for tea.

When she took the dress home, the girls assured her that Bright Sun never carried dresses of this superb quality, they left that to the exclusive couturier area.

'Also *blue,*' Averil queried meaningfully. 'Blue for true love?' she looked slyly at Honor.

'It's to wear to the Hings',' Honor said inadequately and a little uncomfortably.

'Of course, dear. I'd also forgotten that you were already "married". No need to advertise any more.' Averil's voice was a little edged. Honor often heard an edge to Averil's voice when the girl spoke to her.

The next day Mr Hing crossed the floor to repeat how honoured the family was to have Miss Jason and Mr Rowan take tea with them.

'It is my delight,' bowed Honor; she was learning quite a few Cantonese courtesies like that.

Kit was delighted, too.

'Yes, yes, go,' he said eagerly, 'it all helps.' At Honor's raised brow he had tacked on: 'Helps Danny, of course.'

Though she could not see how, Honor agreed.

The afternoon chosen for the visit was a Wednesday. The little girls were home from their school on that day, so Honor would meet them. Hong Kong schools, she had learned, were sadly insufficient, so several selected schools closed down for an entire day during the week to make room for an "outside" class, while others functioned in two sections, morning studies for one set of pupils, afternoon studies for another set.

The little Hing girls attended a school that held no classes on Wednesday, so it was Wednesday that Honor came out in her new blue dress, ridiculously nervous as to what Hugh Rowan would say about it. As though it mattered what he commented, she tried to steel herself, and anyhow, he probably wouldn't even notice.

But he did, and he said the same thing that Averil had, and Honor writhed much more than she had with her flatmate.

'Blue,' he drawled, 'for true love?'

Something inside Honor made her remind him sharply: 'I'm married.'

'What has that to do with true love?'

'They're generally coupled automatically.' She was getting into his big car now.

'Generally,' he agreed blandly. 'Fasten your seat belt—this is Hong Kong traffic!' He released the brake and edged into the buzzing street.

It took a long time to break away from the city proper, then once away new busy centres occurred every few kilometres, slow-ing them up again. But at last they left it all behind them and began climbing a long hill.

Hugh stopped on the way and pulled into a traffic refuge.

'Perfumed harbour,' he indicated, and pointed to the scene below, the same scene as from the Odetta but from a different angle, and framed just now in swimming blue haze, since for the first time for weeks the weather was unsettled.

He drew Honor's attention next to the many Hong Kong islands.

'The gems of Hong Kong,' he told her. 'That one is Cheung Chau, where the Bun Festival is held. Pink sugar cakes rise up in mountains, and there are many lanterns, fireworks and much lion dancing. Further out' . . . he pointed . . . 'is my aunt's island.'

'Lee Fin.'

'Yes.'

'It has a festival, too?' asked Honor.

'Only a small one. All these places have festivals, but Lee Fin, being tiny, has only a minor one. Theirs is the Umbrella Festival. Umbrella making is the only industry on the island.'

'Rain umbrellas?' she queried.

'All-weather umbrellas, but never in

124

dismal Western blacks. Butterfly colours for both sexes, and dream designs. Each small manufacturer tries to outdo the other. You simply must buy a Lee Fin umbrella when you go.'

'This week . . . if I agreed . . . I believe you said.'

'. . . Yes.' There was the slightest hesitancy. But at once Hugh Rowan began indicating something else.

'What's that small island?' interrupted Honor. She pointed to a darkly wooded rise rather nearer to the harbour entrance yet at the same time well away from any of the obvious boat routes.

'Oh, merely some insignificant atoll,' Hugh Rowan said at once, following it with a revving once more of the engine. Again they climbed the long hill. Then:

'This is the Hing house.'

'Oh . . .' was all Honor said.

She had expected something superior from Mr Hing, and Hugh Rowan himself had spoken of a 'mansion'. But she had not anticipated this.

The edifice was almost a palace; there were seven in the Hing family, but Honor, even at a quick glance, could see that the house could have accommodated seven times seven.

Hugh must have read her thoughts, for he said: 'In past years not only the direct family lived in a house but the indirect as well.'

'Mothers, sisters, aunts?'

'Yes, and often more distant than that.'

'Even then there would be space left over,' she commented.

'That would be desired by all. If you look closer you'll see there are many courtyards, that rooms are grouped around these courtyards. They were built that way to keep the family together yet still separate. When we go inside you'll see that the Hing parents have their own private courtyard, the children theirs, and that there's one waiting for each of the children personally when they grow to young womanhood and have their own suites.'

'To which they will eventually return with their husbands and families,' suggested Honor.

'Hopefully so, since it would give much pleasure. But husbands and families are not so easy to come by these days. Actually it's becoming increasingly hard to marry off a daughter. You see, through the years tradition has established that the young man must provide a background for his wife equal to the one her parents did, but the prevailing hard times are no longer good for that.'

'He could pretend,' Honor said without thought.

'. . . As you are pretending?'

'I . . . Oh, you mean for your aunt.'

A pause, then: 'Yes, my aunt.'

Rather hurriedly Honor raced in with: 'It seems an admirable arrangement for a house this size. The children grow up but remain close.'

He nodded. 'It's also an arrangement universally used. The young, struggling husband will bow and say that his wife is sick for the home hearth, and the parents, though conscious of the real facts, will accept the reason. No loss of status for the young husband, and their child still near them for the older couple. For the Cantonese is extremely fond of his children, and the female children particularly have a deep daughterly piety.'

He pulled up, and said: 'I'll leave the car here.' He got out, came round and opened Honor's door. By that time Mr Hing had emerged from a front courtyard. Mrs Hing was behind him, and to Honor's delight both wore traditional dress. But handsome as Mr Hing looked in his black brocade, and Mrs Hing in her lilac kimono with a silver-grey obi, it was the children, in a little crocodile behind them, that brought tears of pleasure to Honor's eyes. They were dolls, lovely Chinese dolls. Their black silk hair was worn in the traditional Chinese topknot, and they were small replicas of their mother in their identical kimonos, only in melting icecream colours of pink, yellow, green, blue and apricot.

'My daughters,' bowed Mr Hing, and if he felt any qualms at marrying them off in the years to come he did not show it. 'Chiao, Mei, Chi-yun, Wei-ti, Liu. Little girls, this is Miss Jason.'

'Miss Jason.' Their topknots nearly touched the floor of the paved drive.

'Also Mr Rowan.'

'Uncle Hugh.' Forgetting they were Cantonese little ladies, very polite, very proper, the five of them descended on Hugh, miniature Liu placing her tiny slippered feet on his big shoes and begging for a walk, Wei-ti, evidently the athlete, actually climbing up to his shoulder, Chi-yun, extremely small for the middle of the family, hugging his knees, Mei and Chiao nestling under each arm.

'Girls!' It was Mrs Hing, but Hugh stopped her.

'It's my moment much more than theirs.' He frolicked with them, something that Honor would not have believed he could do, or certainly would want to do. He seemed to her definitely not the frolicking sort . . . yet he was definitely enjoying himself.

'Enough!' called Mr Hing presently. 'You know what our visitors have come for. Now attend to it at once.'

He clapped his hands, and the claps must have meant something, for the girls released Hugh and formed into a little crocodile again, only this time they confronted Honor in a horizontal line. When they were perfectly straight they cupped their small palms together and bowed, an even deeper bow, if that was possible, than before.

Chiao, as the eldest, stepped forward.

'Please to take tea,' she said in her high, tinkling little Cantonese voice, and the small five turned and led the way into a room beyond the main court, the beaming parents nodding for Honor and Hugh to follow.

At once Honor was enchanted with the utter simplicity of the room she entered. Apart from chairs for the four adults, five low stools for the little girls and a number of beautifully embossed tables, there was nothing else save the mats on the floor and silk scrolls on the walls.

The small girls had silently gone out, and while they were gone Mrs Hing explained that they were about to perform a tea ceremony for the visitors, an "extra" they had taken at their school, for the ancient Cantonese had had such cultures many years ago as well as the Japanese.

'Only our ancestors did not drink powdered green tea beaten to a froth by a bamboo whisk like the Japanese,' Mr Hing informed Honor, 'rather did they prefer an exquisite pale brew served with a sliver of lime. But the peace and the simpleness was present, and that is why we were pleased when the class opened, and our girls were taught gentleness and vision, which is the purpose of a tea ceremony, whatever nation. That is why we are honoured to show you now.'

A silence crept into the faintly green-dim room, and all at once Honor had the sense of being shut away from all her cares.

The little girls returned, each with her burden, a single exquisite blossom in a delicate vase was carried by Chiao, a Blue Willow pot by Mei, two cups by the third daughter, a cup each by the smallest ones . . . and rather unsteadily. But no mishap occurred, and they knelt successfully down by the low tables and went charmingly through the rites.

It was all so tender that Honor felt a treacherous pricking to her eyes, and for a moment she was afraid a tear was going to plop into her cup of pale gold liquor and upset the balance of the circle of tangerine that the little girls had substituted for lime.

Then a hand pressed her hand, and she felt composed again. She looked shyly and gratefully back at Hugh, and he looked gently at her. They smiled at each other.

'It is over.' It was Mr Hing, and with an effort Honor returned to the present, and to five pleased little girls bowing low in response to the applause. Honor wondered if Hugh had been conscious of an effort to come back as she had. She glanced at him covertly, and decided not. He was praising the children, congratulating the parents. He was as smart and urbane as ever.

'And now,' said Mrs Hing, 'we take

English tea. Oh, yes, Miss Jason, that, of all things learned from the British, is the most memorable to the Cantonese. Tea and cake.' She rang a small bell, and this time two young maids came in, one with a stacked lacquer tray containing pot, cups and cream jug, one with a piled lacquer dish laden with every variety of sweetmeat and pastry Honor could imagine. Forgetting their gentleness and vision, the little girls sat eagerly down and lost no time in enjoying the cake feast.

'Proving your tea ceremony afforded you no vision,' scolded Mr Hing affectionately, 'for you surely will soon be fat as little pigs.'

It was all so pleasant and so informal that Honor had no sensation of time, and she gave a small cry when Mr Hing rose to switch on some lights. She looked beyond the floor-length windows and saw that it was dusk.

'We must go,' she told her host and hostess.

'No, you must wait until we have *deemsums*. I could not let you depart fortified only with sweet stuffs.'

'But——' began Honor.

'You have an appointment?'

'No.'

'Then we shall drink some of our good

132

Cantonese beer this time, eat some *deem-sum*. Man's food will prepare you better.'

'For what?' smiled Honor.

'For the dark night?' suggested Mr Hing jocularly. 'Perhaps for a young man more daring than by day?'

Now everyone laughed, and Honor was grateful for that. She knew her cheeks were burning, and she intentionally kept her glance from Hugh, who seemed to be laughing loudest of all.

The *deem-sums* were many and varied, they ran a gamut from shrimp and chicken to diced pork slivers and delicately cut cheeses. After the sweet feast they did provide balance, as Mr Hing had said.

'I certainly feel better prepared,' Hugh told their host with a satisfied sigh.

'You are now more daring?' Mr Hing asked.

'Very daring.'

Honor knew that both the men were looking with laughter at each other, but she kept her own glance down.

They bade goodbye to the Hings and crossed the drive to Hugh's car. He did not speak as he started the engine, nor did he make any conversation as they began the descent down the long hill.

Then, just as he had earlier, he slid into a traffic refuge. He cut the engine.

Entirely without warning, without preliminary of any sort, he turned in his seat and took Honor in his arms. His sensuous fingers, surprisingly so in such a man, touched the lobes of her ears, the hollow of her throat, traced the delicate line of her jaw. Then the fingers ran through her hair, and with every soft pull an excitement grew in her, an almost intolerable longing to run *her* fingers through *his* hair, to come closer to him as he now was coming closer to her.

She stiffened herself. For all her instinct to respond it was easy to withdraw from him, she found, her nerves were aching so much she could not have borne any more.

At once he released her. He did it so abruptly she slumped down in the seat.

'I was simply trying out Mr Hing's daring young man.' He actually sounded bored. He waited a moment. 'And you?'

'I?' she queried.

'Was it the virtuous wife role you were enacting just now? A matrimonial, not daughterly, piety?'

'If you have the answers, why ask?'

'Oh, I have the answers,' he assured her

lightly, 'but it seems the rest of the circle haven't.'

'The circle?'

'The revolving group in which I've found myself.'

'If the group is so distasteful you could always step out,' said Honor crossly.

'No, I can't do that, I'm now inevitably involved.'

'The firm, of course.'

'The firm?' He seemed surprised for a moment. 'Oh, yes, the firm. On that subject you haven't yet told me your answer as to whether you've decided to go along with the masquerade.'

'I suppose, like your own involvement, it's inevitable,' she sighed.

'Does that mean Yes?'

'Yes.'

'Then we'll cross in two days' time.'

'In your boat?'

He nodded.

'We'll go to Lee Fin?'

'To the island.' He said it a little testily. 'I've already spoken to Mr Hing, anticipating your agreement, and you're excused from work. So is your husband from his department.'

'Of course, you're the man who can pull a number of strings,' said Honor drily.

'Several strings will be enough just now.' He was reversing the car from the refuge again. But halfway out he stopped.

'I'm sorry,' he said deliberately, 'that your stone floated.' She looked at him in bewilderment, and he explained: 'The marriage stone, Mrs Blyth. Remember? I think it rather left the bed of the stream just now. For there was *not* a matrimonial piety in you, was there? Not really. You were actually as breath-close to me in your heart as I'm going to be in one moment to you.'

Before she could answer . . . though what could she answer? . . . he was kissing her, and in the fire and the hard strength of it Honor knew she had never ever been kissed before.

She tried to pull back . . . she tried to cry out . . . she tried . . .

She stopped trying.

She heard him laugh softly, amusedly, and she closed her eyes in angry frustration.

When she opened them again they were edging through the traffic of Hong Kong.

# Chapter Eight

BUT for the old man from whom she bought her paper every day Honor would not have known about this particular time of the year and its history of bad weather.

The old man, always in a frogged tunic and wide trousers with an overlapping front, always carrying a fan and an umbrella as well as his newspapers and magazines, spoke excellent English, and was clearly eager to show Honor how fluently he could converse.

Honor appreciated this, so, after she had brought her paper, she loitered a while to say more than the expected: 'Thank you very much. Good day.' Thus a conversational friendship had grown.

Honor told the old news-seller during their talks that she was going across to Lee Fin, and at once he squatted on the dusty pavement and drew a map. This was the island of Lee Fin, he indicated, patting the grime with his folded fan; it lay past Stonecutters, past Lai Chi Kok, yet not as far as Lantao.

'But,' he demurred, 'when do you go?'

'Soon. The day after tomorrow. Not for long, though. Just there and back. But I thought you might wonder if I bought no paper.'

'It is not the time for such a trip,' the old man reproved. 'You see' . . . with pride . . . 'I keep a record of weather.'

'Typhoons, you mean?'

'Perhaps, even though officially there should be no typhoons yet. But nature herself does not deal in records, she deals in whims. No, rains, I really meant.'

'We can do with rain,' observed Honor. 'Look at that dust!'

'This is true, but the rains at this time of the year can be very bad. They can come with wild storms. They can bring floods. Some while ago rivers even burst their banks, hillsides opened up and houses slid in, foundations were undermined and buildings collapsed. It was not a good thing.'

'No,' agreed Honor, 'but it looks fine now.'

'So does Hong Kong even as the Ty-

138

phoon Imminent flag is being hoisted. Its weather puts on too pleasant a face for too long. Hong Kong is like that. The sky is putting on a good face too long at present. I said this to an old customer last week. He had been consulting me about the weather for some time, as to when the rains could be expected, the big tides, and I said what I have just said to you, that the sunshine will soon break. He even asked me which day, and' . . . with pride again . . . 'I was able to tell him. Here is your change. I hope I am wrong,' he added. 'I hope I will see you again very soon.'

'It will be soon,' Honor assured him, not at all alarmed. 'We're only going there and back.' She smiled at the old man, who gave her a fan wave in return, then went on to the Bright Sun.

When Mr Hing came to speak to her during the morning, Honor mentioned the old man and his weather forecast.

'Yes, that would be our Mr Yok,' said Mr Hing. 'He takes a deep interest in weather. You could say it is his hobby.'

'And he is sometimes right?'

'Sometimes yes, sometimes no. Like all weather prophets. But our Mr Yok does have a devoted following, and is more times

139

than not quite uncannily accurate. For instance, he forecast Typhoon Jane when no one else did. Jane destroyed the homes of thousands of squatters above Victoria. Since then our Mr Yok considers he should be the government meteorologist, not a paper-seller,' Mr Hing smiled.

'He's a nice old man and speaks good English.'

'Who would not be nice and speak good English to such a young lady?' Mr Hing bowed.

'No wonder,' Honor smiled back, 'with such charm, that you have charming daughters.'

Mr Hing, well pleased with himself, went off to examine another display.

Honor forgot about Mr Yok and his predictions, and even if she had remembered none of the group would have listened to her; they were all too anxious to cross to Lee Fin.

When Natalie came back from her Philippines duty she began packing at once.

But—packing? For only one day?

Honor queried this as Natalie took out her airlines bag.

'We're only going there and back, Nat,'

she pointed out, 'so why are you putting in those things?'

Natalie hesitated—but briefly, then said: 'Just shorts and swimmers. While you and Chad go up to see Aunt Lucia and do what's expected of you, I'll be able to explore the island, perhaps bathe.'

'I don't know why you're asked at all,' said Honor. 'Oh, I don't mean that, not really, but it does seem odd when you're not really concerned.'

'Hugh is anxious that there should be another woman present.'

'For a short time only!' scoffed Honor. 'Don't think I don't want you, but——'

'But I would still like to go, Honor,' Natalie said gently, and Honor felt ashamed.

'I want you to come,' she assured the other girl, and the subject was dropped.

The day of the trip across dawned as all Hong Kong summer days seemed to, golden, dry, pleasantly warm in the early hours but promising a far more difficult heat within a short time.

Honor was again confused as to what to wear. She did not know how old-fashioned or how modernly adjusted was Aunt Lucia, what she might smile on, what she might disapprove. Finally she decided that a skirt would be more suitable under the circumstances than the denim jeans she had planned, since jeans would have been better use on a boat.

Idly she wondered what kind of boat.

Chad, waiting with Danny for the two girls in the big vestibule of the Hotel Odetta where the men were staying, but not, presumed Honor, on the superb penthouse floor, had nothing to say when Honor and Nat joined them, not even when Honor wondered aloud whether she should be dressed socially for Aunt Lucia or functionally for the sea journey. Chad seemed, as Danny seemed, simply anxious to get going, and at once the four of them began walking down to the dock where Kit was to meet them. Also, naturally, Skipper Hugh Rowan. Honor's mouth curled as she added him.

Chad did find time, however, to pair off with Honor.

'I suppose we should have rehearsed,' he frowned.

'Rehearsed?' queried Honor.

'This business.'

'Rehearsed a pretence?' she said crossly.

'I wish you wouldn't keep saying that, Honor, it could become instinctive. You might burst it out at the wrong time.—No, on second thoughts a rehearsal might not be wise. It could seem planned.'

'As it is,' she pointed out.

Chad looked disagreeable. 'Just keep your head when I introduce you to Aunt Lucia, and should you start getting any ideas, any righteous thoughts, think about Danny.'

'I'm always thinking of him, why else am I here?'

'Just try to take it as it comes, please.'

'It comes distastefully.'

'Nonetheless try for all of us.' He turned away from her, and the four of them walked together again.

It was hot outside after the cooled hotel, but the walk was not an arduous one, and it would have taken them longer with the inevitable traffic if they had hailed a taxi. Honor wondered if Hugh Rowan was getting his boat ready . . . if Kit, who would not have left the dock after he crossed in the Star Ferry from Victoria, was helping him.

As they approached the wharves Honor looked with delight at a white and tangerine yacht moored to the third jetty.

'It's Hugh's,' claimed Chad enviously, 'but' . . . with disgust . . . 'so is *Cinderella* standing beside it, and it's the poor relation we're evidently being treated to today.'

Honor looked at *Cinderella* and saw that it didn't even rate a name, only a number. After the white and tangerine beauty it certainly deserved Chad's grimace, for it was little more than a—well, a tub. It was unattractive, clumsy, squat, probably, belonging as it did to Hugh Rowan, seaworthy, but outwardly dishevelled, in fact almost ramshackle. Honor turned away in distaste, thereby missing what the rest of them were missing as they turned away too, and that was the number of boxes being quickly stowed at the stern.

Chad, after his first wry look, had accepted the tub, and Danny obviously would have crossed to Lee Fin on a raft. Kit was uncaring, Nat her usual bright self, and Hugh Rowan had come out on the deck to nod them aboard.

'You don't seem impressed,' Hugh said as Honor went past him.

'I only hope the weather is. I only hope it's benignly inclined.'

'How do you mean?'

'I mean is this thing safe?'

'This boat?' he asked.

'Yes.'

'This motor vessel is A1. What makes you enquire about the weather?'

'I've been warned it's a bad time of the year,' she explained.

'By an old paper-seller, by any chance?' He looked at her closely.

'As a matter of fact, yes.'

'Did he tell you——' But Hugh Rowan did not finish what he started to ask. Instead he said blandly: 'So you're afraid?'

'Cautious.'

'Then don't be afraid.' He ignored her correction. 'She's quite all right, if unbeautiful, and just what I need for this.'

'This?' she queried.

He paused, almost as though he was annoyed with himself. Then he told Honor quite sharply to get aboard.

Inside, the boat was even dingier. It was poky and unattractive, and its internal measurements were uncomfortably minimal. Perhaps . . . she thought hopefully . . . it would not start and they could take the white and tangerine beauty.

But it did start, and they moved away from the dock.

For a long while they had to pick a tortuous path between the dense sea traffic, for Hong Kong water busyness was even more formidable than its street counterpart. They had to avoid an incoming liner, dodge the Star Ferry crossing once more to Kowloon, thread between hundreds of sampans and junks, dodge the Macao hydrofoil gathering speed for its journey to 'Little Portugal'. Then at last Honor could look back and see the city they had left behind, Hong Kong with its high-rise hotels, its splashes of parks, its wharves, its irregular breaks of beach and its occasional tree strands.—Also see an insidious yet definite change in the weather.

It had been hot and blue and gold when they had left, but now it was still hot, but the blue and gold weren't there.

It was not actually grey yet, but there seemed a sullen grievance in the air . . . though perhaps it was because Honor was feeling rather sulky herself that she was seeing it like that.

But no, for presently Chad called out: 'It's starting to look dirty, Hugh,' and Hugh Rowan at the wheel nodded briefly back. He was having to concentrate on the bow which seemed to be thrusting in deeper with every moment though still, Honor puzzled, making little progress, in fact . . . several minutes later . . . making no progress at all.

She set her gaze on a distant reef blowing up sheets of spray; it was the only thing to set her eyes on, she thought, for they had lost the sea traffic entirely now, and Hong Kong that had loomed up behind them had slipped entirely away.

She checked her watch, then later checked again, and saw that in the checking time they had not gained, as far as she could judge, any more distance from the reef.

The wind was up now. The sky was not just sullen, it was a fierce black. Presently it began to rain. So Mr Yok was going to be right with his time of the year.

Honor looked towards the reef again. It was *still* the same distance. She supposed she should be pleased over that, it could mean disaster if they came any nearer. But they could still not flounder around like this, not indefinitely. She did not know what fuel Hugh carried, but there would have to be a limit.

It was then she heard the first splutter of the engine. It had been ticking noisily, but still ticking. Now it had a staccato kind of throb.

With the uneven beat came an unpleasant lurching. At times the engine fully recovered and they would win a few yards, then the hesitation returned, the splutter, and they would begin to falter again.

This went on for some time, it seemed over an hour to Honor, and in all that while they still remained the same distance from the reef, almost as if Hugh Rowan was holding them there . . . keeping to a prearranged position.

What position? Honor, straining her eyes to where she believed the coast should be, saw nothing at all, for it was quite dark now, dark at mid-morning! Also the rain had turned javelin-sharp.

She glanced at the men, but they were so full of their own concerns they did not seem conscious of anything. Natalie, too, was undismayed.

Leaving me, Nervous Nelly, Honor thought, because that's what he'll say. All the same, she rose on unsteady feet and crossed to the wheel.

'Can I help?' she asked.

'Help?' Hugh did not look at Honor, but she saw his brows raise.

'The engine keeps failing.'

'And you're an engineer?' he asked drily.

'No, but I can still hear that it's not as it should be.'

'Clever lady. What else?'

148

'It's got dark. I don't know how you can see.'

'I can't,' he told her.

'Then——?'

'But I can remember.'

'Remember?'

'Look, will you kindly go back and sit down!' he snapped.

Honor hesitated. After all, he was the skipper. Then stubbornly she stayed where she was.

'Where are we?' she asked.

'I told you I couldn't see.'

'Yes, but you said you remembered.'

'I was joking.'

'Joking? Here?'

'I should think this would be a time when we would appreciate a lark,' he shrugged.

Honor sighed. 'Where are we, please?' she begged.

'Not quite far enough yet. Almost . . . but not quite.'

'Almost to Lee Fin?'

'To . . . oh, no, I didn't mean that.'

'Then where?' As he did not answer: 'I don't believe you know where. I believe we're lost.'

'Keep believing.'

149

'I also think we're going to swamp,' she added.

'Don't be a fool. Go back to your seat.'

'No.'

'Then sit beside me. You'd better, anyway, because I'm taking her in.'

'In where?'

He ignored her. 'There'll be a bump.'

'Take her in *where?*' Honor persisted.

'Where I have to put her until this passes over.'

'But there's nothing.' Honor, peering through the window, could still not see a thing. He had admitted he couldn't, either, but he had said he remembered.—Remembered?

'Sit down, Honor,' he ordered.

When she did not move, he reached up, grabbed her roughly, then forced her beside him.

The next moment there was a definite scrape and then a sudden shuddering that sent the four passengers behind the wheel bumping to the floor. But Honor did not move, she was too firmly fitted in beside Hugh even to stir.

She felt a wetness, though, the slobbering wetness of angry spray. She heard the hiss of resentful water . . . and then a deep forward thrust into something soft and yielding that seemed to close in on them and hold them there.

At once the shuddering stopped, the lurching stopped. The boat stopped as well.

Honor did not know where they were, she could not see if it was mainland, island, reef. In fact she could not see anything at all but deluging grey, but she could feel that they were held tight.

# Chapter Nine

'WHAT in tarnation, Hugh——' It was Chad, at last bounced out of his introspection. He had struggled to his feet again following the impact, and now he came stamping down to his brother, who was still jammed tight beside Honor behind the wheel.

'What in the name of——'

'I heard you the first time,' Hugh Rowan said coolly, 'and in a situation like this if you can't say something constructive, say nothing at all.'

Chad hesitated, then complied, but he still looked angry. Natalie, Danny and Kit came more slowly after him. It was quite safe to move round the boat now, for wherever the small tub had jammed itself it had done it very successfully; there was not the slightest shudder as the three lined up behind Chad to hear what the skipper had to say.

'Any injuries?' Hugh asked first.

'No,' they all answered.

'Any shock, any reactions?'

'No.' It was chorused again.

'Then my advice to you is to go back, sit down and wait for a rain break. Then, and then only, will we be able to take stock.'

Nat and Danny went at once, and Honor heard their voices speaking quietly together. Kit took longer, but Chad took the longest, and his mouth was set. Honor did not know whether the order had included her, but she could not have moved, anyway, not until he moved first, so she remained there.

The rain had drawn an impenetrable mist around the launch; they all sat in a shrouded world. They could have been anywhere . . . nowhere, Honor thought.

'Does it get you down?' Hugh asked presently.

She looked enquiringly at him.

'This enfolding grey,' he explained.

'It's better than bouncing round like a cork,' she shrugged.

'That could happen again if an exceptional wave burst and we broke free. I estimate we've run into a particularly thick section of sand, *entire* sand. You find such patches around these waters. The sand goes so deep it can't be estimated. You could fall on to it from a fair height and still feel only the impact of a feather mattress.'

'Our impact just now was more than a feather mattress,' said Honor feelingly.

'There were six adult people and there was a heavy boat.'

'Well, the sand may be a buffer, but it can still hold you,' Honor sighed.

'Let's hope in our case until we're entirely free; it would be more unpleasant still listed to one side.'

'How can we be free apart from your exceptional wave, which anyway might never happen?'

'We could float again on a big tide.' —At once Honor was thinking of her friend the news-seller and his 'old customer' who had consulted Mr Yok concerning the weather and *big tides*.—'Such tides, or king tides, *do* occur,' Hugh went on. He sounded very sure of himself, almost as if he had known an end result before an occurrence.

But he couldn't have known, of course.—Or could he? Honor frowned.

They lapsed into silence. Behind them Nat and Danny still spoke in soft voices with occasional interruptions from Kit, but Chad sat apart.

An hour went by. During that hour Honor must have dozed off, because when she was made aware of the situation again it came as a complete surprise. In her sleeping she had missed the gradual cessation of the rain, missed the first thinning of the enveloping grey, and the clear scene now surrounding them caused her to catch her breath in pleasure.

They were on a beach, and it was a very beautiful little beach, whether a mainland or an island beach she did not know yet, but they had definitely not reefed, for even allowing for some sand between rock outcrops on a reef, this sand was far too bounteous for that.

Also, there were trees, a great deal of low, coast-like shrubs, much undergrowth. No, they could not be reefed.

'Are we——' she started to ask Hugh.

'We're on terra firma, islet variety.'

'How do you know?'

He paused briefly. 'I can tell by the beach

contours. If it was the mainland it wouldn't be that shape.'

'I see.' Honor didn't, but she supposed he did. She asked if she could get up now.

'We're all getting up and getting out. We can't wait here and do nothing.' He rose, and called out to the others that they were getting off to explore.

'Explore what?' demanded Chad.

'When we've explored we'll know,' his brother came back. He swung himself off the launch on to the thick deep sand, then reached up and lifted Honor down, and after her Natalie. He left the men to make their own way. He climbed up the beach, and the girls followed.

After the sand stopped, the vegetation began. It was very dense, with regular stands of shortish trees, the same kind of trees that Honor remembered seeing around Hong Kong. She claimed triumphantly that they could not be far from the mainland because of that similarity, and Hugh gave her a pitying look.

'What did you expect? English oaks? Of course the type of tree would be the same, the same for hundreds of miles.'

'Which we are not,' inserted Honor stubbornly.

He ignored that. 'Anyway, it makes no difference whether we're close or at the other end of the world, since we still can't see so therefore we can't be seen in return.' He looked around and Honor looked with him.

He was right; there was nothing at all except sea. No ship on the sea, no boat, no junk, no sampan. Nothing.

'We can't be far though,' Honor insisted. 'We haven't been away all that long.'

'We had a driving wind behind us and we were blown forward for over an hour.' —A lie, Honor knew, remembering the reef that they had been unable to lose.—'A lot of distance can be covered like that. We could be in Communist waters. Or we could be even halfway to Macao.'—Yes, a lie. A deliberate one?

'If we climbed to the top of the island we might see.' Honor pointed to a steep rock outcrop in the middle of wherever they had landed. 'You could see from that height,' she said.

'And do you think you could climb the thing to do your spotting?' Hugh scorned. He nodded to the sheerness of the rise, and Honor reluctantly agreed. The rock ascended almost vertically, and though a mountaineer

156

might have conquered it, Honor knew that she, probably all the others, never would.

'Some passing boat will see us.' She started on another tack.

'Passing from where, passing to where?' he said sarcastically.

'Hong Kong is a busy place,' Honor defended herself, 'there are ships arriving every hour, fishing boats going out, the hydrofoil runs.'

'All on prescribed lanes—even the humblest vessels are controlled up here, even the smallest dinghy. They all know they mustn't encroach on foreign waters—or trouble. No,' he went on, 'I feel this island is outside any of the recognised routes.'

'Then what do we do?'

'What I said, we wait for something . . . an exceptional wave? a king tide? . . . to get us off. Either that or dig the tub out, but I feel even with four men it would be a very deep dig. Anyway, we have no gear.'

'People will wonder about us, come to look for us. Mr Hing——'

'Will assume we're stopping over at Lee Fin.'

'Your Aunt Lucia——'

'Wasn't even expecting us. You see, I never told her because——'

'Because?' she queried.

'There can be disappointments.' He said it quite finally as though to close the subject. At once he went on: 'I think you may as well accept, as Natalie has already accepted' . . . a smile at Nat . . . 'that we're stuck here until we can get off.'

'I can't accept that,' retorted Honor.

'You will,' he shrugged. 'Now we'll see how the boys feel about it.' He smiled crookedly and turned to his brother, Kit and Danny, who had climbed up from the beach by now.

Danny had nothing at all to say, Kit only muttered darkly, but Chad was appalled.

'You mean you don't know where this place is?' he demanded.

'Do you?' Hugh returned.

'No, but I'm not expected to—I wasn't the skipper.'

'No, I was. I was the skipper on undoubtedly the worst day I could have drawn for the job.'

'You know these parts, you must have a feeling, even a remote one, as to where we are.'

'I have little feeling about anything at present, but I will say this: We could be miles away, we could be around a corner, but neither would be any better than the other without any sea traffic to alert.'

Chad was biting his lip. 'You mean——'

'I mean for all we know, or don't know, we could be here for days, months—years.'

'Be serious, Hugh. This is no time to joke.'

'I am serious,' Hugh assured him.

'Aunt Lucia could be dead by the time we got off.'

'Your bad luck.—Also the pretend wife's.' Hugh smiled thinly as audibly Honor caught an enraged breath.

'We—we could even die here ourselves,' Chad said.

'Given long enough time, yes.'

'Then what, Hugh? Hugh, *please!*'

'Now you're showing sense at last,' Hugh drawled. 'Then what do we do, I think you are trying to say. That's what we have to consider, and at once. Consider survival.'

'Survival?'

'Until we get the boat off again we have to consider—and practise—survival. We have to take stock, apportion jobs, carry out the jobs, then be prepared to wait.'

'It's unthinkable!' Chad had lost his eagerness.

'Can you suggest anything else?'

'We're none of us Crusoes,' Chad complained.

'We don't know until we try. And unless we try, we'll perish. It's as simple—and final—as that.'

'You're exaggerating.'

'I'm not. I know these waters, and I know there are dozens of unaccounted-for islands. These atolls, for that's all they are, are unmapped. Probably no one has ever trodden on them before. No one has been interested enough to try. So instead of backing off, Chad, face the truth. And be prepared for work.'

Hugh walked away.

Natalie followed him, and, after a moment, Danny followed Nat.

Honor stood with Kit and Chad.

'It's preposterous!' Chad burst out.

'It's certainly not what I bargained on,' Kit said resentfully, 'one day away, he told me. Why, I could lose my job over this!'

'On your own words,' Honor reminded him, 'Mr Rowan wielded a lot of influence. No, I don't think you'll lose your job.'

'If you ever get off here to go back to it,' retorted Chad darkly. '*Are* we going to get off? That's what I want to know. I wish

160

I was familiar with this darned area. I'm not—I've only ever visited it. It was always Hugh who managed the Hong Kong end of the firm. I had hoped that after I saw Aunt Lucia . . . Hell, I have to get to Aunt Lucia. She's eighty-seven.'

'And every moment counts.' Honor's voice was thin.

Chad turned on her. 'It should count for you, too. I know one thing, your brother won't want to be counting time.'

Honor looked at Kit. Surely he was going to support her now. But Kit was looking distastefully down at himself. He had come in immaculate white drills, and already the rain and sea had crumpled and rough-dried them. He looked dishevelled and disgusted with himself.

'I can't live very long in these,' he muttered.

'You may be living native yet.' It was Hugh Rowan, back once more, Natalie and Danny with him. 'There's nothing of any advantage further in, I mean not as regards a better base. We did find a climbable rock to spy from, though, but the view was the same as here—ocean and more ocean. Apart from its affording a slightly wider aspect we would do better to stop

161

put. We'll go down to the boat, take anything we might be able to use off, then strike camp.'

'I brought nothing,' Kit said querulously as he looked distastefully down at himself once more.

'In which case you needn't forage, you can begin on the camp at once. You, Chad, and you, Danny, can help Kit. Natalie and I will examine the tub and bring off anything that could help.'

'And me?' Honor asked a little nervously, nervous of Hugh's cool control.

'You can check if the spot is suitable,' Hugh said. 'See if it's dry. Free from soakage. Level. Other things a woman knows to look for.' He paused. 'Also see if it's sufficiently roomy.'

'Roomy?' she echoed.

'Extensive enough for one young lady' . . . he smiled at Nat once more . . . 'three men—and a married couple.'

'I—we——' Honor closed her mouth again.

'After that there's a variety of pine in the thicket back there, and young pine needles, if you stack them deeply, can make a fine bed.—Do you and Mr Blyth favour innerspring or rubber, Mrs Blyth?' He was being outwardly jocular but inwardly goading, Honor recognised, and she squirmed. With difficulty she held on to her control.

'Come with me, Kit,' she said deliberately. She even took Kit's hand in her own. She would show this man!

But once away from the group Kit, suddenly aroused, took advantage of her gesture. He pulled her quite roughly to him and his lips pressed down on hers.

'I believe I like you a pagan,' he said, laughing, 'I think I even prefer you gone native. Perhaps all this might be some fun after all.'

'Kit—Kit, stop it!' she begged.

'What's the matter with you, Honor? We're married, remember?'

'You know we're not!'

'Well, they don't know.' He kissed her again.

Honor found herself stiffening in the embrace, she who had loved him near her, loved the circling of his arms, his face against hers.

'What's wrong, Honor?' He sounded angry, and Honor knew she must not go too far, nor let him see how she felt. Anyway, how *did* she feel? It would have been hard for her to say. She only knew that just now she had not wanted the nearness of Kit, she simply did not know more than that.

'It's all been too much,' she heard herself mumbling, and was thankful when Kit accepted her muffled words.

'For me, too. I've never been a pioneer and I don't like beginning now. But if it has to be, then——'

He was stepping forward to her again.

The sound of steps stopped him. Hugh Rowan came through the undergrowth and called: 'Is that all you've collected? You'll have to do much better than that. You need piles of needles, otherwise you'll be feeling all the knots and roots.'

'We haven't collected any yet,' Honor said unevenly, and she knelt down. She began scrabbling among the tree bases. She felt but did not see Hugh's derisive look.

They collected needles for hours. They deposited them at the camp, then, when the pile looked high enough, Hugh called a halt.

'There's sufficient there,' he nodded, 'for five beds.'

In a low voice Honor corrected: 'Six.'

'But surely our bride and groom——' It was Hugh again, smooth, suave.

'I believe,' said Honor, 'that Nat will want me to be near her.'

'Women sticking together,' Hugh drawled. 'Well, if your husband is agreeable . . .'

Kit was acting sulky and said nothing.

'Also, if the "husband by pretence" doesn't object . . .'

Chad snapped: 'Oh, dry up, Hugh!'

Hugh only shrugged.

'Very well, spread the needles. Make a compact job of it so that the wind doesn't blow them away. After that, Nat, to whom I've given the job of cook, has a treat for you. Actually a cup of tea.'

'Tea?' They were all happily surprised.

'I carry a small reserve,' Hugh explained. 'But tomorrow we'll probably be on some tisane.'

'What's tisane?' Kit asked suspiciously.

'A herbal brew. I know a little about the local vegetation and I'll be surprised if I can't find some fern to lighten, if not exactly brighten, our days.'

'Days?' groaned Chad.

Once more Hugh only shrugged.

A fire had been lit, and the can for bailing out was used to boil some water.

'What happens' . . . it was Kit again . . . 'when the water supply stops?'

'It's stopped now. This tea will use up

our last drop of water from the mainland. But there's a source on the island that I've found.'

. . . That he had found, puzzled Honor. She could not remember him leaving any of them, not alone, to find water or anything else.

However, she forgot her wonder in the cup of brew she shared with Danny.

'Tomorrow,' Hugh called, 'we'll look around for suitable shells for drinking. There aren't enough cups to go round.'

They were silent over the tea drinking. What were they all thinking? Honor could not have guessed, but she herself was no longer thinking much of anything, she found she was completely depleted; after all, it had been quite a day. She had a suspicion that the rest of them were feeling the same.

She was astonished to see that dusk was approaching. Could it be as late as that? They had run up on the sand before noon . . . and after that everything had spun by like the facets in a kaleidoscope. Yet night already?

Nat was sharing out bread and cheese, something else that had been brought from the boat. But tomorrow, Hugh called again, the rations would peter out, and they would be on their own.

'Eating what?' asked Chad.

'What you can find. Fish, if you can catch one, rock oysters, berries, perhaps a wild fowl.

'Now' . . . yawning . . . 'I don't know about the rest of you, but I'm hitting not the hay but the pine needles. The way to do it is this: make a hole and bury yourself in them.' He did so, and Chad, Nat and Danny followed suit.

Across the campfire Kit looked significantly at Honor. He used everything he had ever held on her in that long deep look, and Honor would not have been a woman if she had not understood.

For a full moment she looked back at him, feeling Kit's old magic calling her, his magnetism pulling her, she even made a half step towards him, then:

'Goodnight, all!' Hugh Rowan called at the same time as he extinguished the fire.

Somewhere on the other side of the dead blaze Honor knew Kit waited silently in the darkness, but a moment as well as an ember had been put out.

She buried herself beside Nat, snuggling into her needles until they touched her chin.

They were wonderfully soft and gloriously warm. She looked up to the sky, amazingly clear after a day of dark weather . . . yet was that a good sign? When she went back to Kowloon . . . *if* she got back . . . she must ask our Mr Yok. She traced the passage of the moon, counted a few stars, heard even breathing around her.

She slept as well.

## Chapter Ten

HONOR woke up to a feeling of someone watching her. There was no sound anywhere, the sleepers grouped around her made no noise at all, the usual stirrings of the bush were not present. She could have been encased in a bubble, she thought.

She drifted for a while in the deep silence, but the feeling of being watched stopped her from slipping off again. She opened her eyes fully and was surprised to see that it was dawn. She had not thought she would sleep right through the night; she had been comfortable enough, but she had believed that the varied events of the day would have prevented oblivion, yet now the sky was a pearly grey and in places even flushed with rose. She lay quietly in the pine needles, but her glance went searchingly round the group. Then she saw that it was Hugh Rowan who was watching her.

As soon as he caught her eye he nodded, then indicated for her to get up and follow him. Resenting his order but full of curiosity, Honor did so. She knew, anyway, she would not sleep now.

He led her down a path from the camp but did not speak until they were well away from earshot.

'I didn't want to disturb them,' he said, 'hence the furtive retreat.'

'You disturbed me,' she said. 'I could feel your eyes on me.'

'It had to be my eyes, a physical touch might have startled you, you could have cried out, made a noise.'

'And there are no noises,' Honor said wonderingly. 'Why aren't there? Woods are generally full of sound.'

'I don't believe there's any life on this island.'

'Yet there are trees.'

'But the birds obviously prefer elsewhere . . . which could make it unfortunate for us.'

'You mean survival?'

'Yes.'

'I wouldn't care to trap a bird,' she said hesitantly.

'Remind me of that if we catch one and I'll allow you to starve,' Hugh said drily.

Honor did not answer that. She said instead: 'If this was an atoll as you said, there should be coral.'

'There is some coral, not the pretty ornamental variety you're used to, but nonetheless coral.'

'And a ring of coral enclosing a lagoon? For that's what a true atoll is.'

'Would you be surprised if I said there was?'

'Yes.'

'Then why do you think I've willed you awake? To gather more pine needles? No, I thought that you, as star performer in this act, should have the first honour.'

'First honour?' she queried.

'Of bathing. This way' . . . he held up a branch. 'Now what do you say to that?'

What did she say? Honor had nothing to say. She just looked with pleasure. The small circular lagoon that confronted her was quite enchanting.

'An atoll with a wood as well as a lagoon,' she marvelled.

'Also a stream.'

'Yes, you mentioned the stream last night, you said you'd discovered it.'

'That's right,' he agreed blandly, but explaining no further. 'A lagoon to bathe in, trees to supply mattresses, streams to drink from. Nature indeed indulged this place.'

'I agree. You couldn't have found a better refuge if you'd tried.'

'Oh, I certainly tried. I mean' . . . hurriedly . . . 'bringing in the tub was no mean feat. Well, madam, it's all yours.' He nodded to the small lagoon and bowed.

'Thank you. But——'

'But?—Oh, I understand. You naturally want your husband, too? Is that it? You want to share it with him?'

'I do not!' Honor's cheeks were hot. 'But I don't want to bathe with you standing about.'

'Safety?' he reminded her. 'You could get into difficulties and I'd be here to rescue you.'

'The water is shallow,' she said coldly, 'and anyway, I'm a good swimmer.'

'I see. Modesty, then? Will it do if I retreat a few yards?'

'A few hundred yards. Better still, go back and tell the others. We can't keep something like this to ourselves. I shall have finished by the time you return with them. Thank you,' Honor added rather late.

He shrugged, gave a wry grin and went.

'Fetching them,' he warned over his shoulder, 'will only take ten minutes.'

'It will take me nine,' she returned.

As soon as he had gone, Honor pulled off all her clothes. She took them into the lagoon with her and slapped them against some convenient smooth stones. Then she wrung them as dry as she could and spread them as widely as their material would stretch on some bordering rocks. She swam a little, then came back and turned the articles round, then in exactly eight minutes, or so she judged, she dressed again in the half-dry garments. They would be fully dry, she thought, very soon, for it was going to be another hot day.

There were cries of delight over the lagoon when the party arrived, and a roster was made up as to who would bathe, and when.

It took a substantial section of the morning to get through the programme, but after all, as Hugh indulgently reminded them, they had all day. Many days. He looked sideways at Chad.

At the end of the ablutions there was a hot drink waiting. Hugh had found some herbs and shown Nat how to brew them. The result was slightly medicinal in taste but palatable enough, and, refreshed, they began wondering what they could find to eat.

Hugh repeated his doubts as to any chance of trapping a bush hen. Their sustenance, apart from any edible berries, he said, would probably have to come from the sea. He looked across to the men.

'Trapped fish, if we're lucky. Since they haven't been intruded on before, and so have achieved no cunning, if fish do achieve that, there might be an unlucky one, so look in all left-over tide puddles. Then oysters. That's what there is a supply of, because I've seen them, but they're very small, and we'll need a huge garnering. Prising oysters, particularly little ones, from rocks is a long and tedious business. It's also hard on the hands. But that's survival.' He smiled all round, but no one smiled back.

'Edible grasses can be gathered by the girls. If they're doubtful as to how edible they can come to me. Also in their spare time they can find some drinking shells, there should be some around. Well, that fixes the day.'

'What about a distress flag?' asked Kit. 'Something might pass.'

For the briefest of moments Hugh paused. Then:

'A distress flag, of course. Who's the most distressed?'

No one spoke.

'I just asked to give him—her—the honour of making and then hoisting the flag.' He looked around. 'I think we'll give it to the newlyweds, who must be the most distressed of all of us, being obliged to share this idyllic place with four others.'

He smiled blandly at Kit and Honor, but, as before, they did not smile back.

The men found themselves some sharp stones and began the onerous job of prising oysters from rocks. When their hands became numb from the exacting chore Hugh allowed them time off to hunt the leftover tide puddles for anything that could be consumed. Only a small crab was found, but even that was not discarded, and as soon as the pain from constant hammering had diminished it was back to the oysters again.

Meanwhile Nat and Honor collected

174

likely-looking grasses and brought them to Hugh for examination.

He discarded some, saying wryly that if they had planned a wholesale drop-out in the survival class this would have achieved it.

'For after that one . . . and that . . . no one would have survived. But this is a variety of native fennel and should chop up quite tasty, and that fern should make a change from our present tisane.'

'There are also some berries,' proffered Honor, and Hugh examined them.

'A cousin of the small native guava, I think,' he pronounced. 'At least it will provide an anti-scurvy.'

It took all day to gather sufficient food, and by that time the hunters were exhausted.

'We can't keep on doing this,' Chad complained.

'Any alternative?' Hugh asked.

'We could start working on the boat. That makes more sense.'

'You have to eat while you work, remember. Anyway, I fully intend what you propose, but first we have to build up a food supply. A few more days like this' . . . he pointed to the result of their efforts . . . 'and we can turn our attention to either getting the tub out or upgrading the dinghy to hold more than the meagre number it can now.'

'Six?' asked Honor impertinently, for she knew that the small thing would be stretched beyond its limits even to take three.

'Maybe four with luck. In that way the honeymoon island would be catering for its honeymooners as it should be. A moon and stars for two alone. Speaking of newly-marrieds, have the young couple run up the distress flag yet?'

'No,' both Kit and Honor muttered.

'Am I to gather by that there is no distress?—But shouldn't you think of others?'

'Come on, Kit.' As she had the last time, Honor took Kit's arm and led him away. Once out of earshot she said furiously: 'That man, that utterly impossible man!'

Kit was not attending, he was only keen on the distress flag.

'I can't stand much longer,' he muttered, 'my hands are shreds from that oyster business. Oh, why did we start this rotten thing?'

Honor looked at him curiously. 'I've been meaning to ask you that. I *had* to come . . . but why did you?'

'Why—well, I couldn't very well let

you come alone, could I?' Kit was plainly ill at ease at Honor's question.

'Alone with four other people?'

'I just felt I should come. Oh, for heaven's sake, Honor, don't start something . . . particularly recriminations. We're all of us tetchy, and just because of him.'

That, anyway, was something with which Honor did agree, and she dropped the subject.

Previously she had taken off her half-slip. She could almost have known, she thought wryly, when she had chosen a skirt instead of trews yesterday morning that her choice was going to be the right one.

Kit had a thin stick, but when he tried to trace letters on the silk they came out too pale and barely legible even after they smudged the stick end in crushed bark. That gave Honor an idea. She found the berry brush she had robbed earlier and began squashing the berries. It was a complete success. By dipping the stick in the resultant red ink Kit made a fairly good show of their S.O.S.

'If we could climb the big rock we could put it there,' Honor sighed, 'but alas, it can't be done.'

They decided instead on the highest

tree branch they could reach, and secured the distress flag there.

'When I'm down on the beach looking for the shell cups that the big boss has ordered,' Honor went on, 'I'll gather as much seaweed as I can and trace Help on the ground as well. There may be a plane.'

'Or a flying pig,' Kit shrugged. 'No, you want the very top for any messages, Honor, but you'd need to be a rock-hopper to get up there.' He narrowed his eyes at the outcrop.

'. . . Yes,' said Honor slowly. She was looking at a pine that was growing very near to the jutting rock. She had never noticed it before. If one could climb that tree, she thought, transfer to the rock, they could—She had always been a good climber, she recalled.

'If we don't get back he'll be after us again as he was yesterday.' Kit gave a last pat to the distress flag, then began walking back.

Still absorbed, Honor followed him. That tree, she was thinking, I wonder if I could——

Dinner that night comprised oysters and some ship biscuits that Nat had found in the boat.

'Anything else to be found?' Honor asked Nat. 'I'll help you look.'

'You'll keep to the job I gave you.' Hugh came in sharply and authoritatively. 'Nat and Nat only is cook. You will not go near the boat.'

'But why?'

'Because it's our only way out of here, and for that reason it has to be treated with care.'

'Did you think I would take a rock down and bash it? I'm as anxious as you are to get off. Did you think I'd try to launch it myself?'

'I didn't think anything particular, I simply issued an order. And while we're in this insidious position, orders will be obeyed.'

Honor was beyond reasoning now. She called angrily: 'And what orders will *you* obey?'

'The orders of safety and reason. Now stop arguing. Also change the subject. Nat, pour out the tisane. I must say at least you girls found us some likely cups.'

'At least?' Honor bit out.

She was furious, so furious that as soon as the meal was over she slipped away and went down to the beach.

Instinctively her steps turned to the boat. But she never reached it. A man loomed up in front of her, and she thought at first it was Kit.

But the hand that definitely steered her back in the opposite direction was Hugh Rowan's, and the feel of authority was there.

'I told you this was forbidden,' he reminded her.

'You tell a lot of things!' she snapped.

'A leader has to.'

'Self-appointed leader. Also when does a leader *do*, not just *tell?*'

'Do what? Do this?'

The same as on that night coming from the Hings, only several evenings—and a lifetime—ago, suddenly and breathlessly he had Honor in his arms, and the same as that night Honor felt herself stopping there. She hated herself for it, she tried to break away, but—she stopped.

Next would come his hateful amused laugh, she anticipated, but it did not. Instead he kissed her, kissed her quite gently.

'Go up to your pine needles, little bride, and dream of your wedding night—yet to come?' He raised an enquiring brow.

About to retort something, Honor asked

curiously: 'And you, what will you dream about?'

Now the laugh did come, but not amused, not even bantering, indeed it came so quietly Honor could barely hear it. 'I think,' Hugh said, 'you'll be surprised when I tell you one day.'

'*You* will tell me? *One* day?'

He simply said: 'Come along,' and led her back.

Gradually over the next few days they fell into a routine. The men scraped off oysters and trapped crabs, Honor collected foliage and herbs, and Nat combined the two results to present some quite remarkable offerings.

'How do you do it?' Honor asked, awed, for the oysters that had been growing rather monotonous in their raw state had been presented in a delicious sauce. Nat had flushed and looked away, which Honor decided was more than she would have done in the same circumstance. The dish had been a triumph. Nat had even produced an accompanying flat bread to eat with the oysters.

'Made,' Hugh had told her, 'from one of your garnerings, Honor.'

'All my offerings to Nat were green and leafy.'

'The roots were pulverised by our clever chef,' said Hugh blandly.

Someone else, suspected Honor, was being clever . . . a little too clever. For she had been careful *not* to pull up any roots. Anything she had brought in had been attached to a stem, unattached to any tuber.

She began to watch Natalie and soon saw that although the boat was forbidden to the rest of them, Nat went whenever she pleased . . . and did not return empty-handed. What was in those cupped hands? Honor often wondered. If she wondered, too, why Nat was so favoured yet she had been led away from the wreck, it was not a long wonder. At all times Hugh had shown . . . and expressed . . . a marked admiration for the other girl. For that Honor did not blame him—Nat was a sweet person. But her heart did go out to Danny. Danny had no right to be looking at any girl just now, and Honor conceded that, but her brother was most certainly deeply attached to Natalie.

Several mornings after Hugh announced that there seemed sufficient rations in stock . . . 'in stock' meant a hole scooped in the earth and lined with some plastic sheeting that Hugh had somehow managed to salvage . . . and that he and the men would spend the day on the boat, estimating whether they could release her if they worked deep and long enough; also measuring up and weighing the possibilities of the dinghy as another means of escape.

Honor watched her opportunity to go down to the boat as well. She saw Hugh go to the other end of the beach to comb it for any material that might help them, then wasted no time. There were certain things about which she had to satisfy herself.

While the others argued over something that very obviously none of them knew anything about, Honor edged to the stern where she knew 'things' were generally stowed. She could not have said concisely what she meant by 'things', but she did expect something. Why otherwise had she been steered away from here? Why did Nat come down from time to time?

She stepped gingerly into the tub, but it was so settled she could have been treading on firm ground. She crept to the stern.

There was nothing, meaning nothing visible, but those two planks looked as though they had come up at some time, so she would try them now. Hearing the men still in argument, she squatted down and began to prise.

After she had broken a second fingernail she wished she had brought something to force into the seams. She looked around . . . then stopped her activities. A man's large bare foot stopped her.

Being barefooted accounted for the soundlessness with which he had entered the boat, Honor thought angrily, but how had he got himself so quickly from the other end of the beach?

'I ran,' he said hatefully, reading the question even as it flashed into her mind.

'You mean you raced back here because you had something to hide?' Honor demanded.

'Does it look like it?' Hugh Rowan spread his hands to the emptiness.

'You've removed it!' she accused.

'Removed what?'

She struggled to her feet unaided, and made as though to leave. Anyway, there was nothing left here.

'Not so quickly,' he stopped. 'Why have you disobeyed me?'

'Disobeyed you?'

'I told you to keep away from here, to stop snooping.'

'If Nat does——' she began.

'*I told you.*'

'So I'm expected to obey where she is not?'

'Of course.'

'But why?'

'For the plain reason that we're in a situation here, and in every situation there has to be an authority. I am the authority.'

'But evidently not Nat's, therefore not mine.'

'Leave this boat, Mrs Blyth,' he ordered, 'and don't return until I allow you.'

'Oh, I won't. I'll look somewhere else for what I want.'

She had the satisfaction of seeing him hesitate a moment. So something *had* been taken off.

Before he could answer her she ran up to the camp and got back to the job of gathering food for Natalie to turn into dishes that Honor now felt certain even Nat could not turn out . . . not unaided.

But why? Why the elaborate subterfuge? Why . . . and Honor caught her breath . . . why any of this?

It was at the same moment as that silent

question that she determined to climb the rock outcrop, climb it *somehow*. Find out where they were and from that knowledge why they had come. Why there had been a wreck at all.

## Chapter Eleven

IT was to be days before Honor had an opportunity to try what she planned. The castaways suffered their first casualty, their most valuable one, Honor freely admitted, for cooks were always of primary importance. Their cook, Cook Natalie, sprained her arm.

If it had been her foot, her ankle, Honor could have fetched and carried for her while Nat still performed the magic, the dishes could still have appeared on the bush table that Hugh had contrived to make. But a chef needs hands, both hands, so iron rations were offered once more, since Honor, on whom the cooking duties naturally had fallen, had no idea of turning raw oysters into what Nat had.

At first there was no grumbling. The accident had been a sobering one. It could have cost two lives, Danny's as well as Nat's.

The pair had gone foraging for something different in the diet, with luck a fish, a full-sized fish, not just the meagre small fry that was all anyone had trapped so far. Something, Nat had planned, big enough to stuff.

According to Danny afterwards they had found a rather curious rock formation at the end of the third bay. Within the formation had been a small cave, and in it a smaller cave again, and there, visible from the outside, apparently left over by the last high water, had swum a silver beauty they had known at once they must have.

Ordinarily it would have been Danny's job, for a man was always the hunter, and Honor, when Danny recounted the story, had shivered because her brother for all his slimness was actually substantial, and would never have got out again.

But Nat, small, light, quick-moving, had known it, too, and, anxious to get that fish, had leapt into the first cavern before Danny could stop her. Scolding her, he had passed down the spike he had made, believing she would venture no further, telling her if the fish in the inner cave proved elusive then she was not to persist, for the tide was rising and there might not be much time to get out.

Nat had only laughed and called out gaily that at school she had always been selected to get through the servery windows for goodies, and now, as far as she could see, it was no different, as this fish was a *very* good goody. Before Danny's incredulous eyes she had shown him how she got through narrow spaces. She had not seen what he had: that, because of the peculiarity of the rock formation, the exit would prove narrower again than the entrance, also that getting out would entail a spring from a much lower level since the cave fell steeply away. Finally, and most alarming, that from one of the lower corners the sea at this moment was actually entering, and already the base of the cavern was showing damp.

Danny had leapt into the first cave after Nat, and Honor had had no doubt, for she had seen many exchanges of looks between them, that he would have forced himself into the second space, even if he had lost every vestige of skin during the process, even if he knew it meant certain death. However, that did not happen, instead a freak wave suddenly occurred, one that filled the lower cavern completely and even half filled the first aperture, and where its force never would have dislodged a larger person, it dislodged lightweight Nat. Ordinarily Nat should have been thrown against the walls, cut to pieces on the rough rock surface, concussed, but miraculously she was lifted and washed clean through the hole, something she could never have managed of her own accord, there to swirl round like a cork in the water of the first cave until the water washed out again.

It was from that position that Danny had rescued her, half-drowned, very shocked, still terrified, and with one arm hanging useless from impact with the sides of the hole as she had been swept through.

Frantically Danny had carried her back to the camp.

Honor had at once heated up stones on the fire they kept going to warm the needle bed. The bed was already warm, for pine needles manufactured and retained warmth, but Nat would need extra help against shock. She had bathed Nat's many cuts . . . afterwards Danny's. Hugh had splinted the arm. He had then disappeared to return quite soon with something that he administered to Nat. At once the girl had relaxed, felt easier.

'Do you carry pain-killers around with you as a matter of course?' Honor asked later. She gave him a curious look.

He glanced away from her, but before he did she saw the wretchedness in him and she was sorry she had probed.

'This is something I never thought of,' he mumbled rather incoherently.

'I have no doubt that Nat and Danny didn't, either,' Honor had tried to excuse, but it proved useless.

'It could have been bad, very bad.' His voice was troubled. She had never seen him like this before. She was still curious about the administration to Natalie, but she took pity on his obvious unhappiness and did not question him any more.

The others, sobered by the incident, did not look askance at the unadorned oysters they were called upon to open for their meal. But the day after they did. Feeling she must make some effort, Honor made an oyster stew next, and a very miserable one it turned out, merely rock salt and a few chopped leaves in a pathetic attempt to uplift it. She did not wonder at the luke-warm reception it got. Oh, for even a portion of Nat's magic, she thought.

But help from Nat was not forthcoming,

Nat kept any secrets she had strictly to herself, though Honor did notice once a quick look of enquiry to Hugh. She saw Hugh's brief negating look back. There is something, she thought, there is. For instance, Nat was allowed in the boat, yet I was forbidden. When Nat needed relief for her pain it was forthcoming, but forthcoming from where? Something was stowed away in the stern of that tub once, she thought, I was sure of that, why otherwise was I conducted away so unceremoniously when I tried to find out? Where is the supply of whatever is supplied hidden now, and what game is Hugh Rowan playing? Why is he playing a game at all?

She decided to watch.

Meanwhile the meals did not suit Kit or Chad. They did not suit anyone, Honor supposed, but the others were quiet on the subject.

But, typical of Hugh Rowan, even though he did not comment on the meals as regarded himself he still did not let the matter pass over.

'I've been told that connubial bliss is often based on fellow comfort,' he mused hatefully, 'the way to a man's heart and all that. But your husband doesn't look very blissful today, Mrs Blyth.'

'You seem to be told a lot of things,' Honor muttered.

'True things? What do you say, Kit?' He had turned his attention from Honor. 'Do you find the oyster stew bliss-making?'

'It's awful,' Kit said sulkily. 'I'm not blaming you, of course, Honor, but——'

Chad did not add his piece, but he looked even surlier than Kit did. He got up from the bush table and strode down to the beach.

Honor joined him there as soon as she got an opportunity.

'I'm sorry about the meal, Chad,' she said honestly.

Chad looked surprised and a little ashamed of himself. 'You couldn't help it, I suppose.'

'No, I couldn't. We can't all be born cooks, though perhaps I would make a better show if——' Honor waited, then repeated: *'If.'* She looked at Chad and willed him to look back.

He did look back, first in curiosity, then in enquiry.

'It's this, Chad,' Honor said bluntly. 'Why are we here? *Why?*'

'Why? Well—the result of bad weather,' Chad answered testily.

'. . . Carefully timed bad weather? Timed beforehand?'

'Timed—oh, come off it!'

'I said timed beforehand, Chad, and I meant it. I've been told that unlike Australian weather, which confuses even the experts, Hong Kong weather runs very much to a pattern, that it can be read fairly accurately well ahead.'—Mr Yok, Honor could have added, read this weather ahead.

'Just what are you talking about, Honor?' Chad demanded.

'Frankly that I don't believe that all this is what it seems.' Again Honor spoke bluntly. 'Would your brother do a thing like that?'

'Like what?'

'Like—a wreck?'

'What do you mean?' asked Chad.

'I mean a wreck, Chad. Would he do it?'

He shrugged. 'Hugh would do anything to achieve a result.'

'But what result? Would he want Aunt Lucia's money for himself and not you, for instance?'

'I don't know what you're after, Honor, but no, I wouldn't say that. Hugh has more than enough already, left by his father's side.—Honor, what *are* you trying to say?'

'I've said it. I don't believe all this is what it seems.'

'But you were witness along with the rest of us, we *did* run aground.'

'On a practised island? It was a very efficient grounding.'

'All right then, but——'

'On a very likely day,' continued Honor, 'likely according to a successful forecaster?'

Chad stared at her. 'You're not trying to tell me that——'

'No, I can't tell you because I don't know. But I do know that all Natalie's success, her culinary success later, was not merely because of Nat, and I'm also still wondering where that drug Hugh gave her came from.'

'You mean—a secret hoard?'

'Yes.'

'On the boat?'

'Not any more,' Honor explained. 'He had to take it off.'

'He?'

'Hugh. He saw me snooping.'

'Then where is it now?'

'That's where you can help, Chad . . . after all, I'm going to help *you*. Oh, yes, I know you'll tell me that I'll really be helping Danny, but I'll still be necessary to you later on.'

'If we get off.' Chad ran his fingers through his hair. 'Honor, where are we? Have you any clue?'

'None . . . but I intend to find out.'

'How?' he asked.

'I don't know yet, but I mean to, and soon. But while I'm doing what I plan to do, I want you to keep your eyes open, Chad. Somewhere on this island Hugh has put some necessary things in a safe place.'

'Then thank heaven at least for that, it could be a matter of life or death for us . . . it nearly was.'

'Agreed, and I'm glad he did it, but I'm still wondering why it had to be done at all.'

Honor left it at that and went back to the camp. She knew she had said enough and that Chad would now begin to question a few things.

She wondered as she worked around on the domestic side of their existence, the side that Nat had previously managed, why she had gone to *Chad* and not Kit . . . but she did not wonder very deeply. She was aware now that as quietly and unobtrusively as she could she was beginning to avoid Kit, that any moment alone with him was fast becoming a worry instead of what it should have been, a joy. She did not believe that Kit had noticed this yet, but that afternoon she found she was wrong. She had need to go to the stream for water, and Kit must have seen and followed her, then, when he saw her returning, stepped behind a bush, only to step out abruptly again. The well-timed shock sent the water container . . . the old bailing tin . . . spilling its contents, and she turned angrily on him.

'Kit, you utter fool! Now I'll have to go back for more.'

'No, *we* will go back for more. Honor, you've been avoiding me, running away from me. Why?'

'I haven't. I mean, we're on an island with four other people. It's not as though we're alone.'

'Four other people who recognise us as married.'

'We are not!'

'Who accept us as married.'

'We are not,' she repeated.

'They still accept it,' Kit persisted, 'so why don't you, Honor? Why isn't it you and me together? Why are you going the virgin bride on me like this?'

'It's not the place.'

'You'll never find a better place.' Deliberately he kicked aside the container spilling the rest of the water, and he pulled her to him. His arms were rough.

If she had gone along with him a little, she might have calmed him, even got him to see reason. But Honor was inexpressibly angry, she was furious that he could have followed her up as he had, thrust himself on her like this.

She put both her hands on his chest and pushed him violently away, she pushed with all her strength, and as she ran away herself she heard him swear.

Though she heard no pursuing steps she still kept running, she did not know in what direction, but it did not matter. This island was so small that losing oneself was impossible, one had only to make one's way to the coast and circle it until the camp was sighted. Panting, she kept on, not so much to escape Kit now as to exhaust something in herself, something she could not have explained, something she did not even comprehend. She was out of breath when the sudden vertical wall of the rock outcrop halted her.

She stood and looked at the monolith, recalling her thoughts as to how one might scale it by first scaling its adjacent tree, then transferring oneself across to the rock wall.

Before she knew what she was doing she was hauling herself up on the first bough.

Up, up, up, she went, the second bough, third, fourth, fifth, then when she reached the top branch she found, as she had anticipated, that she could get a toehold of the rock's steep ascent by bending the branch in the rock's direction, a simple procedure by slanting her weight forward, leaning out and making a grab. At no time in her ascent did the fact occur to her that she might climb up this way but she could never hope to descend. All she was aware of was a blind determination to make the rock top, and her determination won. She got there. She looked around. Nothing, she found.

No, there was nothing to see, that is nothing more than she had seen from the ground level. Still only trees, still only beach, still only sea. A sea without any ship on it, any boat or even sampan. She bit her lip in disappointment.

Nevertheless she must be sure, and she pivoted slowly, painstakingly, straining her eyes against the first fading of the day—a silly time to have done a thing like this.

Then a quick flash struck her, a flash

like sun momentarily hitting something in the far distance. Some thing metallic, say— part of a car? Briefly, almost infinitesimally, it had been there.

She stared, blinked her eyes, gave her head a shake, stared again . . . then recognition came flooding over her.

Two weeks ago . . . more? less? she no longer seemed to be able to count . . . Hugh Rowan had pulled into a traffic refuge on the way up to the Hings' as he had shown her the islands of Hong Kong. He had called them the gems.

But there had been one islet he had passed over very quickly, she remembered, very uninterestedly. Of course he had been uninterested, one is always uninterested in something in which one is interested *very much.*

Hugh Rowan had been interested in this islet, interested enough to come here previously to 'practise' something, something that he intended to do in the bad weather he knew was near-certain.

All this shipwreck had been arranged.

Honor no longer asked 'Why? *Why?*' She only rejoiced in the fact that as the crow flew, or whatever birds performed such measurements in Hong Kong, they were near home. That they could be home quite soon. If she could see the coast, the coast could see her. That was being optimistic, perhaps, but someone must look across some time . . . after all, she had . . . and with a distress signal placed properly this time, something metallic, or a flame of some sort, they would have to be discovered.

In her pleasure Honor performed a small jig, and sent a scurry of stones scattering. She almost sent herself as well.

It was only then that she looked down . . . and felt sick. It was much further, much steeper, than she had believed. Also the branch that had helped her climb here was now blowing in the other direction, for the wind had changed its course. Finally . . . and hollowly . . . the initial fading of the day was over—why, it was not far from night.

All at once badly scared, Honor crouched down, holding tightly to a small battlement of rock for support. She must give this some steady thought. But she did not think much, she just trembled . . . trembled at what lay ahead.

Once the first shadows of night began merging, she knew, the onset would be dramatically fast. It seemed to her already that each time she turned her head the outlines had become more blurred. Soon it would be quite black, that dense black that precedes the first prick of stars and the first glimmer of the moon. The darkest part of night. She bit back a little cry of fear.

One thing, it was warm, but she was aware that in the later hours . . . if she managed to stop on here that long . . . a chill would set in, and she was only lightly dressed.

She crouched on, thinking now of Kit. It was only because of Kit she had run up here—oh, she had intended scaling the rock, but if she had not been so disturbed she would certainly not have attempted it at this time of day. No—not day any longer, she saw.

I've been a fool, Honor wept too late. Because of Kit I've got myself into this. A week ago I would not have run away. What has happened to me since? What has taken place?

But though the question was easy to ask, she found an answer not so simple. She crouched closer to the base, took a firmer grip of the ridge of stone—too firm, for it gave way in several places and the sound of the tumbling pebbles unnerved her even more. What, she thought fearfully, if I fall asleep; people do fall asleep in spite of themselves. Will I fall over like those pebbles just did?

She hugged herself closer and blinked into the darkness. She did not dare close her eyes, yet on the other hand if she just stared then the obscurity could become mesmeric, and she no longer would have control of herself. It will be better, she tried to cheer up weakly, when the stars and the moon break through.

She wondered if the camp was looking for her. They would have noticed her absence, but probably shrugged it off as a sudden impulse to get away for a while; at some time every one of them had suffered that. Also Kit when he returned sulky and uncommunicative would be no help.

Later on someone might be dissatisfied and look for her, but who would think to search up here? Again, unconsciously, Honor's fingers tightened, and again some rock splinters slid down.

About an hour went past; she judged it to be that, for a first star came out and it usually took that time for stars to begin. It was a very little star, quite a meagre one, but at least it was something. Honor looked up at it for encouragement until it began to waver mistily in front of her, and she remembered that this was one of the things she must not do.

She sat straight up, very alert, very purposeful, and began counting. She recited a few stanzas of verse.

There was complete silence. Though noises at night can be disturbing, she found this silence unbearable. Unconsciously she strained her ears for those familiar sounds of darkness, slur, slither, sigh, even footfall. There was nothing, not even the distant surge of the sea. The water must be very calm tonight, she thought, not to send out some sibilant reminder.

Her knees began hurting against the rough base, so she changed her position. Although she did it cautiously it still started a fall of stones, and her heart thumped in fear. The second position was even more uncomfortable, but she retained it, and started . . . automatically . . . her listening again. Listening for a twig falling, a stir in the bush below, any sound at all.

In spite of her determination to stay calm in any circumstance, she knew miserably she was losing the battle. A coldness was taking her over, and it was not the cool of night, it was the iciness of fear. If she kept her head she would not fall over, but could she keep it for eight more hours, keep it until light came again? No, she was not as disciplined as that.

Suddenly not caring any longer what she was doing, she got up from her aching crouch. She was crying, crying aloud as a child does when it is afraid, she was stretching out her arms, moving forward a pace.

The step took her straight into a strong, firm grasp, and for a moment she rocked in the grasp, then, as the grasp tightened quite hurtingly, she stopped. She stood still.

'That's better.' It was Hugh Rowan telling her. 'You're all right, but only for as long as you remain where you are. We are exactly eighteen inches from the drop on my side, twelve inches on yours.'

'*Twelve?*' she gasped.

'Be quiet, Honor. Don't move. Don't speak. Presently we'll sit down. Right, are you ready now?' He squatted down first. When he had fixed himself to his satisfaction he reached up for Honor, then carefully lowered her.

'You can talk now. In fact you can cry if you want to. But no sobs, sobs create a hazard. Also an even closer settlement, please. Like this.' He drew her tighter still to him.

Honor felt his chest against her cheek, felt the hair on it pricking her skin.

The meagre star was brightening, a moon was emerging, soon there should be some light.

She sat obediently there, still fearful—yet not now *so* fearful.

She waited for him to speak.


## Chapter Twelve

HUGH'S first words were barely controlled and very angry. He demanded: 'Are you entirely a fool?'

'I suppose I am,' muttered Honor. 'When I climbed up I never thought about how I'd get down again.'

'But you'd been here before, you'd examined the rock?'

She nodded.

'Then?' he asked.

'I did this on impulse.'

'What kind of impulse? An escaping impulse? Were you running away from something and suddenly were halted by this?' He touched the outcrop with his free hand.

'I——'

'*Were* you?'

'Yes.'

'Running from something—or somebody? Don't shrink away, Mrs Blyth, or you'll have us both hurtling to doom. Whom were you running from?'

Honor did not answer, and he gave a scornful laugh.

'No need to act loyal; I know it was Kit, if only by deduction. At the time of your absence he alone was absent as well.— Oh, yes, I watch all your movements. After all, I'm still the skipper, even on dry land. When Kit returned he was alone. He was also sulky, silent—and limping. He'd fallen down, he said.' A pause. 'Would you like to go on from there?'

'I would not. Anyway, you seem to know everything yourself.'

'True or false?'

She did not answer that, but presently she began to speak in a low, resentful voice, resentful at being questioned like this.

'Yes, Kit was with me. Yes, we had some words. Yes, I ran off. But surely that would only be expected of people like us.'

'Like——?'

'Like—newly-married couples,' she mut-

206

tered, more uncomfortable now than indignant, wishing she had not started on this trend. 'Well' . . . defensively . . . 'you said that several times yourself.'

'Yes,' he agreed with wry amusement, 'I said it. But when I did it was in sympathy, not in the anticipation of a battle.'

'It was not a battle,' she retorted crossly.

'From your side it must have been, for there were also a number of scratches inflicted as well as the limp.—Sit still, Mrs Blyth, even if you don't care about yourself consider me. You're rocking the boat.'

'You would be the last person I would want to consider,' Honor flung at him. 'It's you who've done all this.'

'All this?'

'This supposed wreckage on this supposed desert island. For some reason you've perpetrated this monstrous hoax.'

'Oh, so you've found me out.' He said it in mock surprise. He did not seem very distressed.

'Yes, I have. This islet is really only some few kilometres from Hong Kong, not at the end of the world.'

'Did I say that?' he asked.

'You chose the islet because it was one

of the few that would suit your purpose,' Honor continued.

'Wrong this time. It was the only island. I'd exhausted the rest.'

'But why?' Honor asked. 'What purpose?'

'The purpose of truth. My brother's truth, your brother's truth, your husband's. Yours.'

'You bring us all to an island to extract truth!' Honor exclaimed incredulously, not believing what she heard.

'I couldn't have done it any other way.'

'You still haven't done it.'

'No, but I possess' . . . Hugh Rowan smiled thinly . . . 'the means of getting the boat back into the water in a very short time. It only needs some necessary equipment I brought along. I have the power of returning you all to Hong Kong in an hour.' A pause. *'If I please.'*

'You could have done this before?'

'Yes.'

'Then——'

'But first I wanted to throw four people together and see honesty emerge at last.'

'You wanted that?'

'Yes.'

'How power-drunk you must have felt!' she said bitterly.

'Not felt, feel. I'm still in the same position.'

'But you're not. I know now where we are. Just over there' . . . she went to indicate, but remembered and stopped herself . . . 'is the mainland. It's the road up the long hill to the Hings'.' She looked triumphantly at him.

'Clever you. But meaning?'

'Meaning we're *not* lost.'

'And meaning?' he persisted.

'That we can signal and be free.'

'Don't be a fool,' he said again.

'But—but I saw a flash. The sun on the metal of a car, probably.'

'Quite probably. But there would be no sun flashing on metal from here.'

'We could contrive it.'

'I hate to disillusion you, but you have your solar directions all wrong, where this islet is geographically placed we could never do that. Also who would be looking back to here?'

'You and I looked,' she pointed out.

'You looked because I drew you into a traffic refuge and showed you something. But who else would look? Be honest. Answer that.'

She did not answer. She warned him

a little hysterically instead: 'I'll tell the others.'

'And do what? Start a mutiny? What would happen then?'

'Let's hope,' Honor said recklessly, 'we would eliminate you.'

'And with me all hopes of ever getting off here. Yes, I mean that. You could actually remain on this islet . . . eating oysters . . . for the rest of your life. Also, though I believe you already suspect this, I've concealed away some rather necessary things, things you would never find.'

'Dietary additions, you mean,' said Honor bitterly. 'Drugs.'

'So you guessed.' Honor knew he was grinning now by the inflection in his voice.

'I knew it wasn't a stray peppermint you were giving Nat after the accident. I also knew that although I never matched Nat as a cook I wasn't that bad.'

'I agree. It's remarkable what a few packets of Cordon Blue magic can do.' Again she sensed his grin.

'How long did you intend to keep us here?' she asked.

'That should be how long *do* I intend? Present tense, not past.'

'But you couldn't——'

'I could.'

There was silence for a while. Honor broke it.

'Because of you Danny and Nat might have lost their lives,' she reminded him. She was sorry the moment she said it, she recalled his last reaction. However, it was true, and if it disturbed him then she was not sorry, she was glad.

'Yes,' he agreed tersely, and in spite of herself Honor bit her lip.

Another silence, and this time Hugh broke it.

'Since you've pieced half of it together I'll tell you the whole. I selected this islet after a great deal of elimination. It had to satisfy quite a few requirements: isolation, inaccessibility, the unlikelihood of anyone coming here, the right beach for grounding and then getting away again, most of all water. Food didn't matter. Actually I wanted us to fend for ourselves.'

'You considered that character-making?'

'Of course. And' . . . Honor sensed that hateful grin again . . . 'not such a hardship after all, with Nat to help.'

'Nat knew?'

'Yes. I practised the ditching until I could have done it in the dark, which was what

I did do in the end, having also selected the weather.'

'On Mr Yok's advice.'

'Yes, our Mr Yok told me the day that summer would break.'

'He could have been wrong,' she pointed out.

'He could, but he wasn't. If he had been I would have found something amiss with the tub and returned to the dock to wait for another time.'

'There was plenty amiss with the boat *at* the time, was that rehearsed as well?'

'It's wonderful,' Hugh Rowan smiled in answer, 'what you can pretend when you try.'

'The weather has been fine since,' Honor murmured.

'Yes, our Mr Yok told me that, too. The break, he said, after that fine weather, and then——'

'Then?'

'That's yet to come . . . if it does come. But you're diverting me, Mrs Blyth, let me get back to my account. Because I wanted nothing grave to occur, I carried emergencies. When you started to pry, I removed them from where they were and put them in some other place. In time, when I considered it was long enough, I was going to halt the charade.'

'When was that time to be?'

'When several people learned honesty, not evasion. I said that before.'

'You brought us all here for a lesson,' she observed. 'Couldn't that have been done in a more comfortable place?'

'An extraction, not a lesson. I had to extract a truth.'

'And now I've spoiled it. Because I will spoil it. I'll go back to the camp and tell them what you've contrived.'

'They'll listen,' he shrugged, 'but they'll have only one real purpose in view, that of getting off.'

'Which you don't intend yet?'

'Not until I consider the time ripe.'

Honor thought about this for a while.

'You're making the men work manually every day on the boat,' she accused.

'It won't hurt them. Toil never does.'

'But it won't free the boat?'

'No, only I . . . or the elements . . . can do that.' He gave a low laugh.

'I think,' said Honor in a trembling voice, 'you must be the most hateful man in the world.'

'Maybe . . . but you still won't be treating me like you treated your husband,' he suggested thinly. 'In our present predicament that would be very ill-advised.'

'I can't stop up here all night with you,' she said.

'Not propriety, surely?'

Honor bit her lip. 'I can't stop because I—I would fall.'

'Then you shouldn't have come, should you?'

'You shouldn't have come after me.'

'It was either that or be messed about with a broken body. I preferred the first.'

'As a matter of interest,' Honor asked, 'how did you get up here?'

'A bush ladder I'd built myself.'

'A ladder? Then——'

'Oh, no,' he said at once, 'not in that hopeful voice. It's a one-person ladder only, also I'd never attempt it at night.'

'It was night when you came up,' she reminded him.

'Semi, not full like this. Also I climbed *singly*, a very big difference. The ladder is a makeshift article and less than stout.'

'Would you descend it by yourself, though?'

He considered that, then said: 'Yes.'

'Then go. Please leave me. I just can't bear the thought of you being here all night.'

'You've left out being here *with me* all night. I'm sorry about that. Had I known I would have substituted your husband instead. Yet I feel by the way he looked he would have declined.'

'How long until light?' Honor asked desperately.

'Hours yet.'

'I'm cramped intolerably,' she complained. 'I'll never last out.'

'You'll last out, Mrs Blyth, because I'm not letting you escape me like that, not like hurtling to your death.'

'Yet it would suit you, surely?'

'Strangely enough, no. Perhaps, like the song, I've grown accustomed to your face.' He spoke lightly, but somewhere Honor heard a different note in his voice.

'Be serious,' she said thickly.

'If I concede to that it could be a catastrophe on this narrow ledge.'

She set her lips. Oh, how she loathed this man! But for all her hate she was still thankful for the steadiness of his arms around her, the rock-like security of his grasp.

'Suppose you fall asleep?' To her dismay her own lids were growing heavy.

'I won't sleep,' he assured her.

'You'll wake me if I do?'

'Sleep, little one,' he permitted, and his voice seemed to come from a long way off. Honor tried to stretch her eyes wide, but they started closing.

Presently the stars blocked out, the moon. Everything blurred.

Several times in the night Honor stirred, looked up, felt the encompassing of strong arms, then slept again. On the last occasion she could feel his chin resting on the top of her head and she asked drowsily: 'Kit?' not knowing what she said.

Hugh did not answer, but she would not have heard him, anyhow, she was asleep again.

When he awoke her, though, she had her full senses, and she asked: 'Is it daylight? Is it all over? Can you see the way down?'

'It's not dawn. Dawn is a long way off. We're in trouble. Take a look at that sky.'

Honor looked up and gasped. It seemed impossible that the stars and the moon that had canopied them before had disappeared so completely. They were in a black, black world.

'Is there a storm coming?' she asked.

'Probably, if it follows what Mr Yok forecast. But it's the wind I'm most concerned about.'

'There is no wind.'

'It's beginning. Listen.' He stopped talking while she did, and she heard a first stir, an insidious rustle, almost, she thought, as though a giant was awaking and stretching his sleep-cramped limbs. 'That,' said Hugh, 'is how a typhoon sounds when it first begins.'

'But it's not the season,' she reminded him.

'It's the rim of it, and even if it were not there's no law in nature to forbid a freak occurrence out of time.'—Mr Yok, too, had said that, Honor recalled.

'In which case,' Hugh went on, 'we have to get down at once.'

'We can't! It's too dark, we wouldn't be able to see.'

'Perhaps, but at least it would be a try against being hurled over. We're vulnerable here. Can't you understand? We're the highest peak of the islet, and a typhoon would blow us off as easily as a breeze blows a thistle.'

'You said yourself the improvised ladder might not bear two weights.'

'We still have to do it,' he insisted.

'Do you know which side you put it?' Honor asked.

'I can feel around, but it will mean you waiting by yourself.'

'I did before.'

'Not in a rising wind, because that rustle is already gaining force. Feel it.' He released her for a moment, and she was shocked at the strength that had built up.

'You see,' he said, 'there's no choice.'

'I see. What do I do, Hugh?'

'Grab on to anything you can. This bit of rock will help. Make yourself a dead weight. Pretend you're attached here, immovable. You're good, I think, at pretending. Don't stir.'

'No,' said Honor.

He released her entirely now, and the wind that had augmented unbelievably from the breeze of a few moments ago whipped around her with a biting sharpness. But for the fact that she dug herself in at once, Honor felt sure she would have rolled off with the first blast.

After a few more blows there was an abrupt abatement, and she remembered reading how typhoons, cyclones, hurricanes always do this, they take a breath for a second onslaught, then, refreshed, they begin again, only stronger, fiercer, wilder. She braced herself for the next attack, and presently it came shrieking at her. Somewhere in the woods around them she heard a tree fall.

Now she held on for grim death, pretending, as Hugh had suggested, that she was immovable. The wind cut through her. She felt but did not see Hugh crawl back to her and add his weight to hers.

'I've found the ladder. Luckily it's on the lee side, if there is a lee side, and it's still standing. At the next abatement we'll start down.'

'I'm afraid,' she whispered.

'What do you think I am?'

'Hugh, I can't leave here!'

'The wind would soon see to that,' he said grimly.

'I can't leave here of my own accord.'

'Then it will be of mine, because you are *going*, Honor, *and now*. It's easing. The third blow will blow us both off however hard we resist.' He got to his knees, dragged her to hers, then began a painful scrape across the rock face.

The only thing that could be said about that nightmare few yards was that the wind left them alone. It was still resting for its next blow when they reached the ladder.

Hugh put his foot on the rung first, then forced Honor to place her foot after him. Barely had they stepped down than the third wind burst.

This spasm was like none of the others, it cut viciously at them, it roared, screamed, shouted, lifted them, threw them back again. More trees were uprooted and the sound as they crashed downwards was like discharging metal. They could not descend, they dared not ascend; Hugh simply held on to the flimsy ladder with one hand and with the other he gripped Honor. Honor knew his fingers must be agonised, for his grasp was agony to her. They rocked and swerved and teetered and rotated crazily for five appalling minutes, then, the same as before, the wind cut off.

At the same time the improvised rope section of the ladder gave way, but fortunately at first on one side only. Hugh, still holding Honor, slid down now, all caution gone, his only anxiety to reach earth.

The fourth wind broke when they were some six feet from the base, and with it the other side of the rope collapsed. They fell in a heap at the bottom, miraculously not on rock but on flattened undergrowth, and there they lay breathless until the last wind blew itself out.

Even after that they did not get up. Instead they lay on the undergrowth. They lay side by side until dawn.

At the first buttering of light Honor opened her eyes and looked around. She had been drifting, not sleeping, and yet, she realised, she must have slept, for she was now in Hugh Rowan's arms. If she had known, she would have withdrawn, for, in spite of the fact that he had saved her last night, she deeply disliked this man. She bit her lip and wondered how she could extricate herself and not rouse him. He was breathing heavily, still probably exhausted. After all, he had made a tremendous effort, accomplished an unbelievable feat. Looking up at the rock towering above them, she wondered how he had held her as he had, how when the ladder had given way he had impelled her with him to the one patch at the rock base where they would not be injured. No . . . reluctantly . . . she must not move, she must let him rest.

She looked around and was shocked at the devastation. Barely a shrub seemed to be standing, and what few had resisted the blow had hideously criss-crossed. The lower vegetation was ravished, crumpled, split, ruined. Any berries or flowers had been stripped off. It all made for unbelievable debris. Disaster was the only word Honor could say to herself.

Even though she did not speak it aloud, it must have reached Hugh subconsciously, for he stirred, opened his eyes, and, because she was the nearest thing to him, he gazed unwaveringly at her.

'Is it that bad?' he asked.

'How bad?'

'As bad as your face is telling me.'

'Look for yourself,' she invited.

'I prefer it here.' He had not unclasped himself from Honor. 'All the same——' He let his gaze rove round.

'Mmm,' he said.

Honor was trying to wriggle away from him, but either intentionally or unawarely he was still retaining his grasp on her.

'Is that all you have to say?' she snapped.

'No, it's bad, but what did you expect? Also it will recover. Nature always recovers. It's the man-made things that suffer in something like this.'

'As the camp will have suffered?'

'A few pine needles scattered around, my table knocked into pieces.' A shrug. 'That's one advantage of having little, you have little to be destroyed.'

'*They* could be destroyed. Nat—the men. A lot of trees have fallen. One could have fallen on them.'

'If they hadn't the sense to find a safe spot before the height of the blow they deserve a knock. Nonetheless we'd better get down there.' He disengaged her, got to his feet, leaned over and pulled Honor to hers. Then they began picking their way through the battered woods to where they had positioned the camp . . . or that was what they thought.

'Would Hong Kong have had this?' Honor asked as they went along.

'Superficially only. Just as in our Australian cyclones only the eye is the real damage area, and we were that eye, not over there. But I do think it might have started the rains, and when it rains, the real rains, I mean, for Hong Kong even a typhoon takes second best.'

'Second worst, you mean.'

'Yes.' He pushed aside a fallen branch for Honor to pass by, 'second worst. There was a bad catastrophe some years ago. The rains were so heavy the mountain above Victoria gave way. There were several losses.

It was a horrible time.—I say, this isn't so easy, is it?' He stopped and stood looking around him at similar scenes of flattened growth and debris, destroying any guide lines they might have had.

'Thank heaven,' he shrugged, 'it's a small island and we can walk around it, otherwise I doubt if we would ever find the camp.'

They plodded on through more ruin. They could not see one familiar aspect, not even the central lagoon or their stream, but they, Hugh said, were probably concealed by fallen logs by this.

'The only thing is to descend to the beach and start walking round,' he said presently.

'But where is the beach? Any of the beaches?' Honor asked.

He hunched his shoulders and suggested that they walk until they found an intact tree, if one remained, so he could climb it and look out.

Finding a tree took a long time. It seemed to Honor that only rocks had withstood the blow. But they did find one upright one in the middle of a battered stand. It, too, was badly bent, but it would still afford better viewing than the ground.

Hugh climbed it, and let his gaze circle round. He took much longer than Honor expected, and when he jumped down again he seemed puzzled.

'Don't tell me the sea has been blown away?' she asked.

'No . . . it's there.'

'Did you see the camp?

'Of course not.'

'Then——?'

'We go this way.' He began walking again, only this time so quickly that Honor had to run to keep up with him.

In a few minutes they emerged to a beach, which beach they could not have said. It was so littered with crashed logs, blown shrubs, battered leaves and under-growth that no sand could be seen. But at least it was a guide, and they could begin to circumnavigate. Somewhere along it, perhaps still sheltering in some cove, or even a cave, they would find the others. Also the boat. Honor said this aloud, not noticing that Hugh did not reply.

It should not have taken them long. Honor herself had walked round the island in less than an hour on many occasions.

But that had been on sand, not wreck-age like this. Often they had to move large objects to get past, always they had to climb over or crawl through.

All the time they kept their eyes open for the others, and every now and then one of them would shout. But nobody came out and there was no answering cry.

The only cry came a long time afterwards, when, exhausted, they reached their starting point again. It was Hugh's cry, and it was not for the others, who, he had impatiently repeated to Honor all the way, would have holed up safely somewhere, it was for something that had missed Honor—but not missed him.

They had circled the island, trodden every beach, but had not seen it.

The boat, their only communication, was not there any longer. It was gone.

## Chapter Thirteen

'ARE you sure that it was here that we grounded?' Honor asked nervously, nervous —and a little puzzled—at the anger in Hugh's face. He would be desperately worried and upset, she was herself, but why this rage?

'No, I'm not sure, but what difference does it make? We've circled the islet and it's not anywhere.'

'Was it deeply jammed?' she asked.

'You saw it for yourself.'

'But not knowledgeably. I took your word for it, though I admit it did feel very firmly set.'

'It was,' he said. 'Digging would never have removed it. I only gave the fellows that job for something to keep them fit.'

'Digging with their hands!' she exclaimed.

'With anything they could find.'

'Knowing it would still make no difference!'

'That's right. Only I could have moved it off with a right tide and a special contraption.'

'Yes, you said all that before.' Honor's voice was ice. If Hugh heard the chill he took no notice.

'Yet,' he said frowning, 'the tub has gone.—My God, if I thought——'

'What, Hugh?'

'If I thought they'd found what I hid and floated the boat and abandoned us——'

'They wouldn't do that,' she said.

'Then where is it? *Where?*'

Honor stepped away from him to move up the littered beach and shout: 'Cooee . . . are you there? . . . where are you? . . . come out!'

'You'll have to scream across to the mainland,' Hugh, following her, said furiously. 'When I meet up with Chad I'll . . .' He stopped short. He bent over, picked up a piece of wood.

'What is it?' Honor asked.

'Nothing—nothing.'

'*What is it,* Hugh?'

'It's a timber scrap from——'

'From the boat?'

'Yes.'

'Then they couldn't have taken it?'

He did not answer at once, but when he turned to her his face was drained of colour. 'They could have,' he reminded her in a low voice.

'And—this happened?'

He nodded, and looked down again on the wreckage. Honor looked with him. There was no denying that it had come from the tub.

'Danny,' she said helplessly. 'Danny.' She added: 'Little Nat.'

'You've missed out the two others. My brother Chad. Your husband, Mrs Blyth.'

'Chad and Kit,' she echoed him.

'Your husband,' he said again.

'. . . Except,' Hugh Rowan came in after a long pause, 'I don't believe that happened at all. I can't think they found where I planted the wherewithal.'

'Nat could,' said Honor.

'Nat was only up to the boat hideaway. She broke her arm after that, and things had to be fetched, not looked for.'

'Then if so . . . and heaven grant so . . . where are they? *Where are they*, Hugh?'

'Some place. They have to be. Look, we'll call again together.'

They took a deep breath and shouted.

'Cooee . . . are you there? . . . cooee . . . where are you? . . . come out!'

And at the third desperate summons they were successful. There was the sound of voices distantly answering, debris crashing as someone broke through, and after that they were six once more.

Disjointedly the quartet told their typhoon story.

The winds had caught them unprepared, they related. Within minutes . . . less . . . everything they had collected for their use and comfort had blown away, not a pine needle left, no food stock, no table, no carefully collected shell cups, just nothing at all.

'We made for a cave,' Danny related. 'We reckoned at least that couldn't be picked up and flung aside. We've not come out since.' He looked around in puzzlement. 'Isn't this where we beached the boat?'

Hugh did not answer. He listened while Chad corrected: 'No, the next bay,' and while Kit called: 'You're three bays out.'

Then: 'You're all of you wrong,' Hugh announced. 'But don't ask me where. Just let me tell you how we stand, because you have to know it soon. It's this: Wherever the boat was, it's not there now. It's gone.'

'Gone!'

It took a long while to sink in, to be fully absorbed. Even when it was realised there was still a hollow silence for several minutes.

Chad spoke first.

'Is it anywhere in sight?' he asked. 'Have we any chance of retrieving it?'

'It's not in sight and there would be no chance, I think. Look at this.' Hugh handed round the piece of wreckage. 'The tub must have been bashed to pieces when the core hit last night. Anyway, to my mind it would be a boat no longer.'

'No longer,' broke in Chad again, 'but— but that means——'

'It means we're stuck here, doesn't it?' It was Kit.

'You were stuck all along,' Hugh pointed out.

'But with a boat—with a ray of hope——'

'Now you have neither,' Hugh said calmly, 'and as your wife, Mrs Blyth, will now tell you, quite unneccessarily so. Go ahead, please.' He looked at Honor.

'But——' Honor was instinctively stepping back. Now that it actually came to it she would never have said what she had told him she would. She withdrew again.

'Go ahead,' Hugh ordered harshly. 'Tell them what you discovered yesterday, then relate the whole story.'

'No,' she said flatly.

'Do it, I say, then after you've finished I'll begin what *I* have to say.'

'Hugh——' she began.

'Do it!'

In a low voice Honor did.

'We're not far from the mainland.' They were her opening words, and they caused an instant outcry.

'How do you know?' . . . 'What mainland?' . . . 'How long have you been aware of this?' . . . 'Does anyone else know?'

Only one of the questions was answered, and the reply was Hugh's to the last demand.

'Yes, I know. I've known all along.'

'All along? You mean you were aware where we were but you never told us?'

'I mean that.'

'How did you know?' It was Chad. 'Oh, I realised, of course, right from the start that you were familiar with these waters, but how did you know in weather like that to come to this unmapped, unheard-of place? Had you been here before?'

'Many times before.'

'But why? Why?'

'To check the reliability of the water supply—we had to have water. A few other essential details.'

'That almost sounds' . . . Chad's voice was cracking . . . 'as though you arranged it all.'

'You're quite right.' In contrast to Chad, Hugh's voice was calm. 'I arranged every detail.'

'The wreck?'

'Pre-planned. That was why we used the old boat. The weather was pre-planned, too, as far as God and our Mr Yok could assist.'

'But why? *Why?*' That question came again and again, and from the others as well as Chad. Only Honor and Nat stood silent. Silent and waiting.

Hugh spoke at last.

'It was done in the pursuit of truth,' he said, 'a truth I believed would emerge if we remained here long enough.'

'It seems,' Chad burst in, 'we may remain here for ever, even if we're in reach of the coast. Unless' . . . hopefully . . . 'you saw to that, too, arranged for us to be "rescued" in a given time?'

'I made no such bargain. I anticipated that when the truth did emerge we could emerge, too.'

'The boat——?'

'The boat, though ditched, was not as irrevocably ditched as you all thought, in brief I could have got you off at once. But Nature played a trick on me, and now we're really marooned. We could be here for ever.' He looked narrowly at his brother. 'So no need any more for truth?'

'You must be crazy!' Chad flung at him.

'For what? For loving Aunt Lucia?'

'I loved her, too, she's my aunt as well, remember.'

'But even more than your aunt, you hope, your way out?'

'Way out of what!' demanded Chad.

'Come off it, Chad, come off it . . . *and come clean.*'

'I've done nothing,' Chad muttered.

'We'll ask someone else about that.' Hugh glanced intentionally at Danny.

'No . . . no.' It was Chad again.

'I think,' said Hugh, facing Chad once more, 'you'd better begin. Start when you, not your misguided young friend here' . . . another glance at Danny . . . 'deliberately manipulated the firm's books.'

'I didn't,' Chad refused, 'and, anyway, I was a partner, not a mere employee.'

'A junior partner and a dishonest one. Because I was away more than I was present you had a free hand. You were trusted. But the usual attractive salary paid to junior partners was not enough for you, so, to put it bluntly, you helped yourself to more. Much more. Then you got frightened and blamed someone else.' A pause.

'Now I come to you.' Hugh turned directly to Danny this time. 'You're not entirely hopeless, you know, so why didn't it ever occur to you, even being lamentably inaccurate and slipshod, that the amounts you were regularly short of couldn't possibly have sprung from only your source?'

'I—I don't know,' Danny blurted miserably. 'I've never been clever, not like that. Perhaps it did happen, but I wasn't confident of myself, and—well, I liked Chad. I liked him very much. We were friends.'

'You must have liked him blindly to let him manipulate you as he did. You were a damn fool.'

'But not dishonest?' It was Honor, gladly, proudly.

Hugh turned on her now. 'Not so fast, we haven't finished yet.' Again he concentrated on Danny.

'Even though you freely admit your commercial *in*abilities you must have been strongly aware of your emotional *abi*lities. To be brief, you loved your sister?'

'Always.'

'Yet you allowed Chad to persuade you into suggesting, of all outrageous things, a marriage?'

'Yes, I did,' said Danny wretchedly, 'but I doubt if I would have gone through with it, even though I knew what lay ahead of me—I mean, not at the end. But it didn't have to come to that. Honor had already married. She'd married Kit, so there was no question of anyone else.'

A pause, much longer than any of the other pauses. Then:

'*Presumably* not.' It was Hugh.

'Presumably?' Danny was staring at Hugh in wonder.

Hugh said: 'I think now we turn to our final pair. Note that at no time has Nat entered any of this. She came because' . . . a smile, the first smile for a long time, at Nat . . . 'I begged her.'

Honor kept her glance from Danny. How was he taking this? she thought. She had known without being told by her brother what he felt for Nat.

Hugh was speaking again, speaking blandly. Honor hated him when he used that smooth, urbane voice.

'First we take our bridegroom—not the pretend one but the real one. How all our sympathies have gone out to him, marooned on a romantic island with his beautiful new wife *plus a company of four others*. Especially after he'd only made the journey to support the wife while she supported her brother. Greater love and the rest . . . even though he did it for a price.'

'For a price?' It was Honor. This was going too far! She turned blazing eyes on Hugh.

'A price. A very good price,' Hugh re-affirmed. 'Kit Blyth came to Chad and said that unless he was paid he would tell

Aunt Lucia, or at least see that she was told. Chad, who had no money despite all the money he'd had, came to me, of course. Go on, Blyth, tell your wife the rest.'

'No, no, don't,' Honor said angrily. 'It's not true ! I don't believe it. Kit only came with me because——'

'Tell her.' Hugh's eyes were only on Kit.

'It's no good, Honor.' Kit's voice was low. 'I did accept some money.'

'You demanded, not accepted, it,' said Hugh, but Honor was not listening.

'You mean money for not announcing we were married when Chad took me to his aunt? When' . . . Honor took a deep breath . . . 'we were *not*.'

She was aware of Danny's quick incredulous look at her. At Chad's complete surprise. She was not conscious of Kit's reaction, for she had turned away from him. Nat, of course, already knew. As for Hugh . . .

'At last,' Hugh said, 'we have the truth.'

'Was it that important?' Honor heard herself asking hollowly. 'Important enough to bring us all out here, possibly to perish in the extracting?'

'Yes. Truth is always important. Isn't your brother's innocence important?'

'Of course, but——'

'Isn't Chad's deception of a frail old lady important?'

'More remotely, yes,' she admitted.

'Isn't your boy-friend's preference for gain important?'

'Yes . . . no . . .'

'Isn't your own self-regard?'

Honor said coldly: 'You've left out Hugh Rowan.'

'Very well, then. Isn't *my* love important?'

'Have you any love?' she asked contemptuously.

'Yes,' he said without preamble. 'For you.'

At once he went on as though he had not said that.

'Now we have examined all the things that led up to this unfortunate position, that has finished up, as you just said, Mrs—no, Miss Jason, isn't it?—to our fate.—But' . . . looking beyond the group, looking past the coast . . . 'it seems we're not going to perish after all. If you turn to the east you will see that help is coming, that someone either has missed us and come after us, or simply chanced on us. Take your pick. For, my five fellow shipwreckees, we're about to be saved.'

They all turned and looked, and there in the distance but plainly coming nearer was a boat. Even as they stared with relief tinged with disbelief someone on the boat raised a flag.

That started an immediate response. Kit waved, Chad climbed a rock and held up his hand, Danny took Nat's arm and ran down to the water's edge.

Only Hugh and Honor stayed where they were.

'Not quite the curtain I planned.' It was Hugh speaking drily.

Honor did not answer. She could feel a pain in both her palms where her fingernails were cutting deeply in.

'Have you any love?' she had asked contemptuously.

'Yes,' this man, this unspeakable man, had said. 'For you.'

Gradually the boat came closer. Hugh set the men clearing a space on the littered beach.

'Why, it's the *Tak Fu,*' read Honor. 'It's One Million Blessings!'

For a moment Kit straightened up from his task and looked across at her.

The *Tak Fu,* on Hugh's advice, did not venture up the beach after all. It was a luxury boat, not an expendable tub, and it was a mystery to all of them how it had got here.

They soon learned. The skipper held up a piece of wreckage, *their* wreckage. He called out that he was on charter and had seen the sad remains, and at once asked his passengers' permission to freelance around for a while to see if he could find from whence the shattered boat had come.

Some ten feet from the shore the launch engine was cut to a low throb, and the boat and its occupants waited for the marooned victims to wade out. Eager hands pulled them aboard. The cook, who had been busy below, came up at once with steaming mugs of tea and large meat sandwiches. Never, thought Honor, joining in, had food tasted better.

She found herself standing near Kit . . . or had he come to stand near her? By mutual, unspoken consent they both moved away together.

Kit spoke first.

'Well, it's all out now, isn't it?'

'Yes, Kit.'

'I don't know what to say, and even if I did know how I'd say it.'

'Then don't.' Honor managed a small smile.

'Is that because of the pay-off I accepted?'

'No, Kit, I think it's just because of us. There wasn't ever any future, not really.'

'No, Honor, there was none. I learned that on the island. You avoided me on the island. There were all the ingredients, but you turned away.'

'But did you want me not to?' she asked.

'I—I——' he stammered.

'*Did* you, Kit?' she insisted.

'All right then, seeing we're still playing the truth game, no. *No.* I did fall for you, Honor, but then, as Averil always tells me, I never fail to fall for a new woman.'

'Averil——?' she queried.

'I knew Averil . . . knew her that way, the love way, long before.'

'And love her now?'

'Love her always,' Kit said in a low voice.

'Then, Kit?'

'It's not so easy. We're both of us the same kind. The unsure kind, you could say.'

'Not the faithful stone sort.' Now why had she said that, why had she remembered the old outback story that had so fascinated the Bright Sun audience?

'Stone?' puzzled Kit.

'It's nothing, Kit. And please stop being solemn. We met, we believed we fell in love, we fell out again. Now we're friends. It's as simple as that.'

'Except that you weren't being paid for something that should carry no payment.'

'I was in a way,' she said. 'I was being paid by a chance for Danny.'

'What will happen now?' he asked.

'To Danny? To Chad? I think we should leave that to them and think about us. At the end of this journey we'll get off and I shall go and re-book at the Hotel Odetta, later get my things from the flat, or have Nat bring them.'

'And me, Honor?'

'The last time I saw Averil she seemed at a loose end. Whoever was—well——'

'Currently in favour?'

'Yes, Kit, they weren't in favour any more. Go back to Averil, Kit. Have your quarrels if you must, but always make them up before you start filling in time like you filled in time with me. For that's all it was.'

'Honor, I didn't, at least I didn't think of it like that. I swear it.'

'Tell Averil,' ignored Honor, 'to do the same. Also, Kit dear' . . . she became aware of someone turning sharply away from her as she said that and she saw it was Hugh Rowan . . . 'good luck.'

Only Kit heard the 'good luck'. Hugh had gone to the other end of the boat.

It was pouring rain as they dipped into a wharf at Hong Kong Island, raining as they got a taxi, raining all the way to Kowloon.

It rained all that week.

## Chapter Fourteen

HONOR moved back into the Hotel Odetta. It was an expense, but it would not be for long. She had told Mr Hing that she would be returning to Australia as soon as he could make arrangements for someone else to take over the display.

Mr Hing was very sad to hear Honor's announcement. He said Mrs Hing would be sad, too, and the small girls most un-happy. They had been rehearsing a little play for the next time Miss Jason and Mr Rowan came for tea.

'I'm sure Mr Rowan will go,' encour-aged Honor, 'and no doubt my replacement would love to, that is if you cared to invite her.'

'It would be a pleasure, only there will be no Australian replacement. You are our Australian sprig of wattle, none other. I am certain Mr Rowan will feel the same.'

Honor was less than certain. She had not seen Hugh since she had arrived back. Of course she had known he had only been exhibiting his usual misplaced sense of humour when he had replied to her question as to whether he had any love that quiet: 'Yes. For you' . . . but she still had expected . . . she had expected . . .

. . . What *had* she expected?

Meanwhile it kept raining, and there were new fears about the hills above Hong Kong Island, years ago the rains had been so terrific that landslides had scarred the picture-book background to Victoria, and there had been a bitter loss of life.

Honor would have liked to have asked our Mr Yok about the weather . . . asked him a few other pertinent questions, but it was too wet to stand on a pavement; all one could do was to crouch under an umbrella when one crossed a street or withdraw as far as one could under an awning when one waited to cross. Her hotel window that had gloriously captured Hong Kong harbour now only captured streaming water, and grey, grey, grey.

The only bright things that emerged from the thundering deluges were the umbrellas. Was there anything more attractive than Cantonese umbrellas? Cornflowers, carnations and chrysanthemums spattered over oiled silk took to the streets, and even the men sheltered under brilliant blues, greens and golds.

Thinking of umbrellas made Honor think of Lee Fin, where they had been supposed to go but had never gone. She remembered Hugh Rowan saying that the only industry was umbrellas. Perhaps the pink waterlily umbrella she was putting up now had come from Lee Fin. She would have asked Hugh had she seen him, but she did not see him. Nor Kit. Nor Chad nor Danny. Nor, after she moved out of the unit, the girls. Nat, she could not see. Nat was on duty again, fortunately so, for the Philippines was out of the rain radius. Apart from the Bright Sun girls and the hotel staff Honor saw nobody, but she supposed that when the weather cleared . . .

Saying goodbye to Nita had been simple. The two girls had smiled, shaken hands, then easygoing Nita had excused herself to go out for supplies.

'If it rained *deem-sums* it would make sense,' she had grumbled as she had bundled herself into a dripping coat, for the coats never had time to dry.

She had left Honor with Averil.

A little awkwardly Honor had asked: 'Av, why didn't you tell me?'

'Tell you?' queried Averil.

'About Kit,' Honor explained.

'What was there to tell? He was just one of our crowd.'

'But *your* one of the crowd, just as you were *his*.'

Averil had looked up quickly at that, but all she had said was: 'It's history now.'

'No, it's not, Averil. You see, he still thinks it today.'

Another sharp look, then: 'Honor, what is all this?'

'Nothing, really, the nothing I was to Kit, the nothing Kit was to me.'

'If you mean all that's happened was only a game you played to help your brother, I was told so before.'

'I didn't mean that,' said Honor. 'I meant *us*. Kit. Me.'

'But you did like each other,' Averil had said unevenly.

'And like each other now. But only like, Averil. For myself, on my first plane trip, on my first visit to a foreign land, I certainly did like Kit. I suppose you could say I would have been the same with anyone.'

'Kit isn't anyone,' said Averil in a low voice.

'I know that, Averil. Kit is very dear. I realised that when he said what he did.'

'To you?'

'Yes . . . *but about you.*'

'What did he say?' asked Averil.

Carefully Honor had looked back and told her. 'Kit said: "Averil always tells me I never fail to fall for a new woman." He also said: "I knew Averil the love way" . . . then: "I love her always." ' Honor paused, then repeated: 'Kit said: "I love her always." '

'Kit did——'

'Yes.'

'And—and you? How did you feel? How do you feel now?'

'Averil, I said my liking-only piece before,' Honor smiled.

They had grinned at each other, a little uncomfortably at first, and then easier, friendlier.

'What will you do, Honor?' Averil had asked.

'I'm working out a few weeks with Mr Hing, then I'll go back to Sydney. But not until I see Danny, of course. He hasn't been across from Victoria since we got back. The rains, I suppose.'

'. . . Yes,' Averil had said, and had Honor looked up she would have seen Averil's little smile.

They had parted good friends, and Honor had gone back to the rain, to seas of umbrellas, to a windowfull of grey every night.

During the heaviest of the downpours the Star Ferry was cancelled, and because of street congestion the under-harbour tunnel closed. But Cantonese life was too pulsing for the two cities, Victoria and Kowloon, to be separated for long, so as soon as there was a slight diminishing in the rain records, both ferry and tunnel functioned again, and Honor went across to see her brother.

She had thought Kowloon's rain traffic intimidating, but Victoria's seemed even worse. In the end she decided wisely against a taxi . . . rickshaws were definitely out in weather like this, both for the customer and the puller . . . and voted for a tram. A tram at least had a fixed path, and could not weave in and out of the drenched, slippery streets. Rather wet, but safer, Honor climbed up the leaf-green, four-wheeled double-decker.

The fare was ridiculous, only five cents for the best Hong Kong panorama even a millionaire could ask. The fourteen-kilometre track travelled through some of the densest population on earth, and certainly in Asia, past the Suzy Wong districts, past markets, resettlement estates, the lot.

At Wanchai Honor scuttled out and ran to the canopied pavement. From there she progressed beneath verandah awnings to where Chad and Danny had taken a bachelor dig. She smiled a little, thinking how it should have been Danny who had braved the rains and sought her out, but that was Danny.

She climbed the flimsy stairs and knocked on a flimsy door. She had been here before with Nat. She waited. At a second knock she heard steps on the other side. Chad opened the door.

Chad was completely unexpected. Honor had thought he would have returned to Australia by now, or that his brother would have kept him somewhere near to him where he could keep him under his eye. But on that subject, where was Hugh these rainy days? She never ran into him at the Odetta.

Silently Chad stood back for Honor to come in.

They faced each other a little awkwardly for a moment, then Chad dived behind a screen to ignite a match and put it to a gas ring. Very soon afterwards he came out with tea.

'Come to drum me out, Honor?' He opened a packet of biscuits and put some on a plate.

'Oh, Chad, don't go on like that!' she begged.

'It's only what I deserve. Stripped of the medals I don't have, drummed out.'

'And instead of that?' Honor asked.

'I'm being sent back to Sydney to pick up where I left off. Put on trust again. I wish he wouldn't do that.'

'Who—Hugh?'

'Yes. Why can't he kick me out?'

'Perhaps he loves you,' she pointed out.

'Why do worthy people love unworthy people? For instance, you love Danny.'

'Danny did nothing,' Honor insisted.

'He certainly did that,' Chad agreed iron-ically. 'In a way I prefer my own devilry.'

'Devilry is the right word,' Honor nod-ded. 'Will you do it again?'

'That's a funny question to ask me, knowing what I am, but—no, no, I won't. Though, believe me, coming clean at last is not what you decent people deserve.'

'What do you mean, Chad?'

'In a way you and Hugh have both been to blame for us. To blame for the fall guy that was Danny, the big mistake that was me.'

'Perhaps, but I think it's all going to turn out right.—Well, isn't it?'

'You mean will I, or won't I, do it again? No. Never. All that is past.'

'Will your aunt be very disappointed that there's to be no wife?' asked Honor.

'Our Aunt Lucia died the week we were on the island, Honor,' Chad said gruffly, and Honor sensed he was not far from tears.

'Oh, Chad, I'm sorry!' she exclaimed.

'She was old and tired—too old and too tired for a rotten deception. So Hugh knew best, didn't he, when he changed his mind and arranged something else. He also knew something else . . . and this is ironic. Aunt Lucia had *no* money for all my pains and schemes, she hadn't had any for years. Hugh was financing the island. He was keeping her.' Chad actually managed a sheepish grin, a crooked, lopsided twist of his down-turned lips.

He poured more tea, then said: 'In short, in every way I backed a wrong horse, and I'm glad it's all over now. I'm looking clearly at things for perhaps the first time in my life. With Hugh, even though he'll be far away, to keep his eye on me——'

'And Danny beside you,' reminded Honor.

'But Danny won't be beside me.' Chad looked at Honor in surprise. 'He's not going back. Didn't you know?'

'You mean Hugh no longer wanted him?' A slow anger was building up in Honor.

'Oh, he wanted him, but Danny wanted something else.—Some*one*, I should say.'

'Yes, Natalie. It was unmistakable. So *that's* the reason Danny has been pushed out? To make room for Nat for Hugh Rowan?'

'Oh, for Pete's sake!' Chad exclaimed.

'No, for Danny's sake, Chad. Danny loves that girl.'

'That girl loves Danny.'

'But your brother Hugh——'

'Honor . . . Honor, are you entirely a fool?'

Honor did not answer him. She said instead: 'Where is my own brother?'

'Luzon.'

'Luzon?' she echoed.

'The Philippines. He's with Nat. She has relations with a deal of influence in the airlines, and Danny has been given a job in the ground controls. A loss for Hugh, for in spite of himself Danny did have capabilities, but a gain for the air line. For he'll have Nat to keep him at it, something he always needed, not a sister figure.'

Honor remembered her stepfather and his '. . . right girl might help' . . . and she nodded.

'But if Danny told you all this why didn't he tell me?' she asked.

'He probably has, my letter has only just come.' Chad handed it to Honor.

It was too brief for a letter, it was only a communication.

'Have been given a job here, Chad, so celebrated with a wedding. *Mine and Nat's!* The girls know and no doubt have passed it on to Honor' . . . Averil hadn't, Honor thought . . . 'so now I'm telling you. The very best to you, Chad, like I'm getting. Your turn next? D.'

'Danny is only twenty,' Honor said uneasily.

'What of it? Marriage will make him. Also some men need someone with an extra year or so.'

'Yes, I suppose you're right. But——'

'But, Honor?' asked Chad.

'But I think I'll go home.'

Honor crossed and kissed him, and left.

When she descended to the street she saw it was still raining, but that the drops were only thin pencils now, not javelins. If it kept this up our Mr Yok would be back on the pavement with his newspapers again.

*And I'll be his first customer*, Honor thought.

By the time she got back to Kowloon the rain had ceased altogether. Umbrellas were furled, and people were looking happily up to the first blue patch of sky for a long time.

Honor walked round to where Mr Yok had his stand, and was pleased to see the old gentleman in his frogged tunic and wide trousers with their overlap in front. He stood with his fan, his umbrella and his papers, eager to renew his acquaintance with his

254

old customers after the rain delay. As usual he gave his full attention to each buyer . . . and a little more than that to Honor.

'It is good to see you safe and well,' said Mr Yok, bowing. 'I was right, was I not, when I warned you about the weather?'

'You were, Mr Yok. You were also right when you advised Mr Rowan.'

Mr Yok paused, but very briefly.

'Ah, yes, Mr Rowan.' He bowed again.

Honor, who had intended to pursue the subject, pin Mr Yok down, changed her mind. What good would it do her, anyway? Hugh Rowan already had admitted the whole affair had been prearranged. Also now another idea had come to her, not an idea so much as a—pre-knowledge. She knew in this moment—all moments, she supposed, but particularly this moment—that she must go back to the islet again, go just once. She could not have given a reason, it was simply a certainty inside her.

But the weather . . . she must be sure of that.

'Is the rain gone, Mr Yok?' she asked.

'Yes, indeed. Gone until next season. Also no more typhoons this year. We had only the outer arcs of the blow here, the big winds were over the sea, but we are safe now for a long time.'

'Then it's correct to go on the water?'

'You mean in the water to swim?'

'On the water in a boat,' she explained.

'You cross to Macao?'

'. . . No.'

'Then you take a harbour cruise?'

'Something like that—only a little further out.'

'Safe as a sweet flower,' smiled Mr Yok. 'All troubles gone. Your paper?' He held it out.

Honor walked off, her mind whirling. What on earth had possessed her to ask such a foolish question, almost as if she really intended to . . . intended to . . .

Yet—she did.

She went down to some private hire boats beside the Star Ferry, and found the boat-owners, after a week of enforced inactivity, very anxious to earn some Hong Kong dollars. Yes, they knew the small islet she described. They had never been on it, but they knew it. Yes, a trip across could be done. Madam must not linger long on the island, though. It was already afternoon, and they must be off the place again before dark, for it was an out-of-the-way route.

Only there and back, Honor assured them. No time at all. She added weakly that she had left something behind her there and wanted to retrieve it. The boat boy selected to take her over looked surprised . . . so not everyone knew about the wreck episode . . . but he asked no questions. Instead, anxious to get going, he helped Honor aboard, and they started off.

Within half an hour the islet was in sight. What a devious route Hugh must have taken before, Honor smiled to herself.

The boat boy circled the atoll, spotted the cleared place where they had been rescued, and ran the boat in there.

'I wait,' he nodded. 'But not too long, please. I do not know these waters at night.'

'Only a few minutes,' Honor agreed, and she climbed up the bank, finding the going much easier now that a lot of the ruin and debris had settled down after a week of hard rain.

As she walked she thought what a fool she was. She had left nothing here, and she had paid all that money and wasted all this time to come back. Come back to what?

To look at the lagoon where the island boss had given her nine minutes to bathe and dress before he brought the others? To climb to the rock outcrop and see at its base the place where she and Rowan had lain side by side on the typhoon night? Lain in each other's arms? Oh, why—*why* had she come?

It was then she heard the motor engine.

In alarm she started running down to the beach again. Surely that fool of a boy had not left without her? She knew he had been uneasy about the time, but he had barely put her off, he should have given her longer than this. At least he should have called.

She called herself. She stood and cupped her palms and shouted. But the sound of the engine continued, and presently, as the boat left the shelter of the beach and reached the more visible outer waters, she saw the wretched outboard with the wretched boy calmly setting back for the mainland.

Then she saw something else . . . *some-one*. She saw a man climbing up the cleared bank, pulling something behind him, making it secure. It was Hugh Rowan and he was mooring another small craft.

She walked down to the beach to him.

'Why are you here?' she called angrily.

'Our Mr Yok told me you would be coming this way.'

'He couldn't have known.'

'He did,' he assured her.

'Why has my boat boy gone?' she demanded.

'I told him to.'

'What have you come for?'

'That's the end of your questioning,' he said forcefully. 'It's your turn to answer next.'

'Answer what?'

'Answer me why you think I've come here.'

'I don't know,' she shrugged.

'Then perhaps you could try this for a reason.'

He did not cross to her, he did not climb up to her, instead he *arrived*. It was all that fast. He leaned down and took her up in his arms.

He held her there a long time, then slowly he let her down. He put his hand under her chin and lifted her face and looked long at it. Then, everything deliberate now, no more that first spontaneous action, he kissed her, kissed her forehead, ears, neck, throat, and at last her mouth.

'When I said that I loved you that day of our rescue, what did you think?' he demanded.

'That you were taunting me, like you often did.'

'I see. Just as when you called Kit "dear", called it in a tender voice, *I* believed something as well.'

'I said that because I was encouraging him with Averil, whom he really loves, not me.'

'Yes, I believe that now, why otherwise would you have come back here?'

'I don't know,' Honor said, 'I just came.'

'So I came after you, to tell you all. Not just bits and pieces, Honor Jason, but *all*.

'You see, I fell in love with a photo—your photo. When Chad showed me the picture of the girl he was going to marry I was angry.'

'Angry?' asked Honor.

'That it should be Chad and not me. I'd been dissatisfied with my brother for a long time . . . at no period did I ever suspect Danny . . . and when I saw that sweet face I—well——' Hugh ran his fingers through his hair.

'But I realised it was his good luck and my bad luck, and that a girl like that could put a man straight.'

'So you decided to accept me?'

'*Enviously* accept you. I was in Sydney

when all that happened . . . but I was back in Hong Kong when the dream broke.'

'Dream?' she queried.

'You. I heard your name, then later I saw you . . . saw you with someone else. I didn't want you for Chad, but I also didn't want you like that.'

'Like girl meets boys?' Honor asked.

'Yes. I think that was the reason I decided to let Chad go along with his deception . . . at least, I let him go along with it at first. Then my unhappiness about his work became a concrete thing. My agent in Sydney wrote me some disquieting news about our financial side, and I soon guessed that Chad was in it up to his neck and trying to extricate himself through Danny, through you, through our aunt.'

'Aunt Lucia had no money,' Honor put in. 'Chad told me that.'

'Yes, and it was a shock to Chad, yet he took it well. But all that was *after*, the hurting part was *before*.'

'Before?'

'Yes, Honor. How could you have allowed yourself to be part of such a scheme?'

'It was because of Danny,' she explained.

'How could you have pretended you were already married?' he asked.

'That was Danny, too. I've always been weak with him, the only way I could fight him was pretend I was no longer available.'

'Pretend wife,' Hugh said.

He had stopped talking now. Instead he was looking, looking long and deeply at her. Presently he spoke.

'You told the boat boy you'd left something behind you. Oh, yes, he said that to me when I paid him to push off.'

'It was untrue,' she told him. 'I'd left nothing.'

'Nothing then . . . but now? This time?'

'What do you mean, Hugh?'

In reply he said gently: 'Once I used extraction, remember? Once I used truth. Now I'm using love. I love you. This is the second time I've said that, but from now on love is to be my only yardstick. I don't know yet if you love me, but the very fact that you've come back makes me think you *could* love me. But I'm not waiting for that, not waiting for anything. I'm just loving you, and Honor——'

'Yes, Hugh?'

'It will be dark in ten more minutes. I've brought rations, so there's no need for foraging, but we will require some needles.'

'Needles?' she queried.

'Pine needles,' he reminded her, 'they make a soft bed.'

'Yes, Hugh?' she asked again.

'A soft *big* bed,' he said.

As they gathered them, new and young and supple after the rain, Hugh spoke about the marriage stone, that story Honor had told in the Bright Sun.

'I'm marrying you tonight,' he told her, 'we're going to the stream and throwing down our marriage stone. If it rises, then the marriage is off.'

'How did you know that Kit and I were *un*married, Hugh, because you did know, didn't you?'

'Right from your first lie. It was written all over your face. That face said No, No, No. Besides' . . . impudently . . . 'would Kit have returned to the camp as he did that day?'

'Like what?'

'Scratched. Limping.'

Daringly, Honor asked: 'Would you?'

'Would I?' He looked at her sideways.

He went to the pile of needles they had gathered and spread them thickly and widely. Across the needles he looked at Honor and she looked back at him.

The final shadow fell. For an hour there

would be dark, and then the moon would come up, the stars prick out. But meanwhile the air was warm and the needles lay soft.

'This is the way you do it,' Hugh Rowan demonstrated, 'you dig a hole then bury yourself up to your chin.'

'Two holes,' reminded Honor.

'One big hole,' retorted Hugh. He held out his arm for her to come and help him.

Laughing softly, she did.